Lies in

You'll enjoy these other riveting novels
by Sharron Frink:

Set on the Outer Banks:
- **Cape Hatteras Castaway**
- **Buffalo City Moonshine Murders**
- **Uncharted Deception**

Southern Stories:
- **Longview Legacy**
- **Saving Madison**
- **Bertie**
- **Prisoner of Experience**

…and if you like thought-provoking near-future fiction:
- **Family Protection Act**
- **Family Protection Act II – The Seed of Life**
- **Family Protection Act III – The Unknown Asset**

all available as both e-books and paperbacks at

amazon.com

please visit *sharronfrink.com* for details

Grateful thanks to my First Readers – my husband Rand and my editor Penny Jeavons – for their editing skills and their patience, encouragement and support of a simple storyteller.

Thanks as well to my growing family of readers and supporters who appreciate reading a good story that entertains without the use of gratuitous sex or violence.

Today, 300 years after his death, Blackbeard the Pirate has today become the symbol – the face, if you will – of the days of piracy on the high seas of the American Colonies. Facts about him are scarce; but tall tales abound. I have taken artistic license in telling this story *(it is fiction, after all)*, but have tried to use whatever 'established' facts were available.

If you'd like to learn more of the story of Blackbeard, I highly recommend **The Last Days of Black Beard the Pirate** by Kevin Duffus (Fourth Edition). It was the most interesting and complete picture that I could find.

This is a novel of historical fiction. Except for the well-known historical figures and places, all other characters, places and events are strictly a work of fiction and the copyrighted property of the author and her overactive imagination. All rights reserved. This book may not be copied or reproduced, in whole or in part, by any means, electronic, mechanical or otherwise without written permission from the author except by a reviewer who may quote brief passages in a review.

Copyright 2018

Lies in the Sand

Lies in the Sand

Lies in the Sand

by

Sharron Frink

Lies in the Sand

Part One

Lies of the Past

Lies in the Sand

Chapter 1

November, 1718

The Outer Banks of North Carolina

Somewhere on Hatteras Island

The gut-wrenching screams were loud, deep and primal - like the howl of an animal who had just killed its first prey, proclaiming to his part of the world that he was now its unquestioned master. But this screamer was no wild animal – this was a man!

All heads turned to stare at him as he stood atop the sand dune with his head thrown back and his arms outstretched to the heavens. Wind gusts out of the northeast were growing more powerful by the minute, blowing sand around him in a whirling fashion, which only added to his look of fearsomeness.

The man was tall and dark; his long, frizzy black hair was bound tightly in the back by a leather cord. His impressively thick beard was loosely formed into two greasy, food-laced braids that hung halfway down his chest. Strong broad shoulders filled his coarse, sweat-stained white shirt as he stood high on the sandy rise, facing the ocean. His daring posture revealed a haughty confidence.

The screamer then began to laugh loud and long; and if that scream had been animalistic, then his laugh was truly demonic. The group of four men nearby turned to stare again, two of them looking afraid, even terrified, at the insane, frightful sounds coming from this apparition. His dark face and intense, savage eyes lent him an almost supernatural look, yielding a truly chilling effect.

"Ah, 'tis only Blackbeard being Blackbeard!" said Willy the Whip (as he was called by his mates). The young man shook his head and waved his hand dismissively as if nothing out of the ordinary had happened. "Think not a thing of it!" He turned up the dark bottle of rum and took another long swig, licking his lips.

Another man added quickly, "The time to worry yourself, lads, is when the cap'n *stops* laughing!" The other two frowned, but reluctantly agreed. Their leader's erratic behavior was legendary, and his sanity often questioned, so they simply added this event to a string of others like it, and then went back to their rest and revelry under the shade of the scrubby trees.

Blackbeard continued to stand facing the wind, his arms now crossed, staring out at the ocean as if daring it to question him. It was a sight that one of the men there would remember all his days.

The four scruffy-looking sailors that Blackbeard the Pirate had brought ashore either sat or lay about on the sand, content to pass around the bottle of rum that their captain had given them as a reward for their hard work. Not a one of them thought of interrupting their leader's maniacal process of thought by questioning his actions. They had seen him casually make other pirate *captains* walk the plank, so they didn't dare.

They whispered among themselves about the hard work of digging that they had just done - and whether or not any of them would live to tell the tale. The rugged wooden chest they'd hauled ashore and then buried for Blackbeard had seemed lighter than it ought, but who was to say what this crazy man was about? Blackbeard had threatened to cut off the tongue (and other various parts of the anatomy) of any man who breathed a word of what they'd done here.

So, the four of them were nervous about the whole situation, wondering if perhaps he would just kill them outright after the work was done. But as the strong rum's soothing effect took hold, the small group laughed, joked, and none seemed to be overly fearful about anything their future might hold. They were pirates: the right-now was enough for them. It had to be.

The imposing figure standing on the dune threw his head back, his large hands into the air and laughed out loud yet again, producing an insane cackle that caused his flunkies to glance his way once more. The youngest one of them said, "I do not know, Willy, that sounds to me like he be puttin' a curse on the treasure box we buried!" That was a sobering thought; Blackbeard was a devilish man, to be sure!

Willy was superstitious by nature, but he was the one in charge of this little group and wanted to appear to be unafraid. "And why would he be cursin' his own treasure box?" he scoffed. Willy would try hard to forget what the man had said, but within a fortnight events to come would force him question that resolve and recall the comment about the curse.

"I would not know," the sailor replied, his eyes large. "But 'tis a strange thing to do and he's scarin' me for sure!"

Willy pointed at him. "Now don't you go actin' like a little girl on us! You want us to tell all our mates that you were scared to death by a man screaming?" he asked, laughing. The others laughed as well and the young sailor looked appropriately chastised.

Edward Teach, known far and wide as Blackbeard the Pirate, was now a man in his prime, but his had been a hard life and the wear and tear of it had taken its toll. He was weary and ready for this part of it to end. He had been dubbed 'Lord of the Outer Banks' up until six months ago, when he had grounded and sunk his forty-gun flagship, *Queen Anne's Revenge*, on an outer bar of nearby Beaufort Island. He was now reduced to commanding only his sixty-five-foot sloop *Adventure*, together with about twenty men.

Lies in the Sand

And it had been a good run, Blackbeard told himself. He had, in the course of less than two years, become one of the richest pirates on the sea, with crew and ships enough to stop all of the ships he might encounter. His fierce appearance and his boldness to attack any ship, no matter the size, had made him the subject of many newspaper articles in both England and her colonies.

His reputation for being bloodthirsty and ruthless was known all along the coastal British colonies, from Boston down to Nassau. However, the truth was that he himself had not actually killed very many people; as his notoriety had grown, so had the tales of his exploits. Many of the ships he confronted simply surrendered when they saw him light the little explosives he'd tucked into his beard braids. That fearful sight, together with his mad screaming and attack without abandon, convinced them that this was no ordinary man they were confronting!

Now his desire was to go back to St. Thomas, and certainly not to spend the winter here in North Carolina. They were currently past what sailors called '35 North,' too far north for this late in the season; he knew it and his men knew it. The storms and cold weather would soon be upon them. Like their captain, his men were tired and unhealthy; the few who had still not abandoned him were loyal, but they had no decent winter clothing, and lately were beginning to grow afraid of his mental condition. Blackbeard had been irritable, restless and was becoming careless as well. About twenty men were all he had left, and those carefully avoided his sullen moods and erratic behavior however they were able.

Today he had accomplished what he had come to this barren stretch of beach to do – bury that chest to keep it safe until he would make his getaway. Then, with as few men as possible, he would retrieve his treasure and steal away south, never to be seen again on this cursed shore.

Only Blackbeard knew the one unique feature which set this particular spot apart from the miles and miles of desolation on either side of it. *When God made the coast of North Carolina,* he'd often told his men, *he must have been havin' a bloody bad day.*

While excellent hiding places were abundant in these Outer Banks, the hunting was poor and clean water was hard to find. Here the land was not hilly and lush like the Caribbean, or flat and pure white like Florida sands, but was instead a pitiful string of scraggly islands where small dunes rolled along like the bumps in a road, one after another. Each storm that swept through changed the landscape a bit, shifting the sandy bumps into yet another temporary, random configuration.

The confluence of cold waters of the north meeting warmer waters from the south made this area of the Atlantic Ocean prone to severe storms and very dangerous to navigate. Shifting sandbars here, combined with the unpredictable currents, could be deadly to passing ships, and many had gone down here, never to be seen again.

But Blackbeard knew that in this *one spot alone* on the shore of Hatteras Island there was a strange, uncanny effect; he had discovered it quite by accident some time back. A bad storm had caused him to lose his bearings, so after it passed he'd come in closer to shore to get a visual read on the land. For some unexplained reason, his compass wasn't acting right, so he took a small boat ashore and tried to get a more accurate read.

That was when he first discovered that something strange was here – some magic or witchery that caused a compass's needle to spin wildly! And the heart of this sorcery, the place where it was the strongest, was in the very spot where he had just buried the chest! He reckoned that it was the Devil's work somehow, but that didn't concern him; the pirate and the Devil were on comfortable terms at this point.

No matter the time of year, this place whispered to him through his compass in a special language that only he could understand. Whatever ancient black art had placed that evil power in these sands, he had seen it only here, out of all the many places where he had sailed.

Lies in the Sand

The pirates learned that the few local Indians had a name for this place that translated roughly to 'the place that steals arrows', and the local tribes avoided the area carefully. So, he knew that the priceless treasure that his men had just buried in these sands would remain untouched until he came back for it, which if everything went according to plan, would be quite soon.

He smiled. He'd made a deal with Spotswood, the Governor of Virginia (who had benefitted himself handsomely by protecting the pirate), for an official Royal Pardon in exchange for Blackbeard stopping his piracy. That pending pardon would clear his slate of all British charges and make him a free man again, without the constant harassment of the King's Privy Council back in London.

His future looked hopeful, and he was ready for retirement. But of late, he had slid back into his old criminal ways a few times, because what pirate worth his salt could pass up an easy target? As a result, his pardon was in question and His Majesty's Navy was hot on his trail, out to get him. This was the perfect time for him to disappear.

But first he had to go to Ocracoke Island, just south of here, to replenish his supplies before making for Jamaica. He'd built a retirement home of sorts on Ocracoke; one of his fourteen wives and a few of his forty children lived there, and he wanted to see them all one last time. But he'd been told in Bath Town that His Majesty's Navy was close behind him, and determinedly hunting him down. So, his retirement would have to be relocated further south, much further. He could always get a new wife… or a few… He crossed his arms and let slip a wicked grin.

After taking care of business in Ocracoke, he would come back here to this devilish place to retrieve his treasure and then go south to retire in the Caribbean anonymously, living as just another spent sailor. He'd sell his ships, change his name, shave his head and beard and then drink rum until some beautiful woman stabbed him in a fit of jealousy while he slept. He smiled at the thought of it. Yes, with the sale of the contents of that chest, he would live in comfort for all the remaining years of his life! And if he grew bored, he could always get 'back in the game,' *for he was Blackbeard the Pirate*!

Blackbeard stopped his daydreaming and returned to the present. He steeled himself and assumed his fearsome manner once more, that terrifying look that often had his enemy surrendering before the battle was even engaged. *Fear and intimidation, the tools of my trade*, Blackbeard thought to himself. *If people only knew that I fought as a last resort! Still, better to be feared than to be loved, as 'tis likely to keep me alive that much longer!*

He turned, signaled to his resting men to come along, and headed for the beach and the small boat that they'd used to come ashore from the *Adventure*. The happy little group of four men managed to get up from the sand and staggered toward the beach, laughing and clapping each other on the back.

With a determined look on his weathered but handsome face, Blackbeard strode purposefully toward the sea, to Ocracoke Island, and to meet his unforeseen rendezvous with destiny.

Lies in the Sand

Chapter 2

The following morning, Blackbeard's ship *Adventure* sailed in from the open ocean through Ocracoke Inlet. He spotted Portsmouth Island over in the distance, but that was not his destination. As his ship passed the mouth of the wide inlet on the soundside of Ocracoke Island, Blackbeard slowed down and made a tactical assessment of the situation. His men would want to begin their revelry the moment that he dropped anchor, so he planned to get his reconnaissance of the island done before settling in.

They sailed around the entire island slowly; the place looked calm and safe enough, so he relaxed a bit and at last headed into the small, calm bay of the village to anchor the ship. He would need to acquire provisions and retrieve his cargo of cotton, sugar, indigo and some cocoa that he'd stashed on this island months ago. Most of that haul was French booty, but it would be worth taking south, as he could always use the extra coin or barter the goods in trade.

November 21, 1718

He and his crew had spent several days in Ocracoke, readying the *Adventure* for the long voyage and repairing the ship's sails with the help of the locals. Today's final preparations would allow them to leave with the second tide tomorrow. Blackbeard looked around from the deck of his ship and laughed. The entire bay shore was trashed with broken bottles and other ship's debris from his men's parties and fires onshore. They had enjoyed themselves!

He retrieved his booty from its hiding place in Springer's Point and then talked to his men about the long journey south. His men had loaded the fresh water in the hold. Tomorrow morning, he would send Willy ashore to obtain the last of the supplies to be gathered for the trip. He would say goodbye and depart Ocracoke for the final time shortly afterward. But tonight, he and his men would have one final revelry with which to remember the British Colonies of the Carolinas!

Unknown to Blackbeard, two small, innocent-looking trading ships had sailed southward from the Roanoke Inlet to their north on that same day, November 21st, making for Ocracoke Island. These ships had been recently hired by the King's Navy for an important mission of deception, and would soon become famous for their part in 'The Battle of Ocracoke Inlet.'

Those two ships made their way south toward Ocracoke and arrived in the general area early in the day on November 21st, 1718. They lowered anchor and kept their distance some way off, just close enough to keep an eye on Blackbeard's ship. Those men could hear the sounds of merriment aboard the pirate ship as voices and songs drifted their way over on the water.

Later that day, Blackbeard was surveying with his spy glass and noticed that two small sloops that looked like trader's vessels had dropped anchor to the west and lay quietly some distance away, near the Ship's Channel off Beacon Island. Using his spyglass, Blackbeard determined them to have no cannons on deck and therefore to not be any kind of a threat. In addition, they appeared to be lightly manned, with only a handful of sailors aboard. He speculated that they might even be friendly and would make their way over soon to share some rum and tall tales with his own men. He dismissed them without a second thought.

When he checked again that evening the small sloops hadn't moved. Still, they toiled with the nets and appeared to be fishermen who posed no danger, so Blackbeard relaxed. The pirates invited some guests from the island aboard the *Adventure* for their farewell party, and soon everyone got down to some serious drinking and rabble rousing, which lasted well into the night.

Meanwhile, onboard one of the small sloops, plans were being carefully laid. Lieutenant Robert Maynard of England's King George's Navy had purposefully chosen these two common-looking cargo vessels for this particular mission in order to get close to Blackbeard alerting him to the threat.

Alongside Maynard's ship, the *Jane,* was the *Ranger*, another small, innocuous-looking vessel commanded by Midshipman Edmund Hyde. Both ships' captains had kept most of their men stashed belowdecks as they lay quietly anchored across the shallows from Ocracoke Island. Lieutenant Maynard knew that his deception would not fool the pirate for long, but he hoped that it would give him just enough time to catch the troublemaker off his guard as they made their approach.

Maynard's singular mission was to capture this pirate and bring him to justice. Blackbeard had been a thorn in the side of the Royal Navy for almost two years now, proving to be both ruthless and elusive. So, strategy and cunning would be needed to catch this one, and Maynard had devised a novel approach. By arriving in the two sloops with no cannon and looking like the other ships around, he so far had been able to get this close to the pirate without arousing his suspicion.

The Lieutenant's plan was laid; his men on both ships readied themselves for the following morning, sharpening their swords and daggers and getting some much-needed rest below decks. Tomorrow's events would determine for certain whether Maynard's plan had been a good one!

November 22, 1718

Early the next morning, Blackbeard arose in a dark mood. He dressed quickly and then walked the deck of his ship. His sleep had been poor and he was feeling anxious for some reason; he figured that it was probably pre-voyage nerves, together with his own pounding head. All of his drunken sailors had made it back aboard, but some still lay scattered about the deck. They had slept where they fell, as if suddenly struck down by a quiet but deadly disease.

He knew that his men were seriously hungover, many of them still asleep in the hold, snoring away. He kicked a few booted feet of those scattered about and heard some moans, but only a handful stirred to life. He laughed; his men had had their fun and thus would be easier to live with on the next leg of the journey. But today their heads would make all of them irritable.

There was barely a breeze blowing; the day was unusually still. All boats would have to be rowed until they could catch either the tide or a gust of wind. The quiet, stagnant air refused to blow away the multitudes of flies and mosquitos; so the bugs were everywhere and biting, which only added to Blackbeard's bad mood and the general meanness of his crew.

He got out his spyglass and again checked the location of those two small ships off Beacon Island; they remained a long way off. He grunted in approval and got about his business. But shortly thereafter, he caught movement out of the corner of his eye in their direction. As he studied them, he saw them quietly raise anchor and prepare to sail out.

As he watched them, the small sloops got underway, turning toward the island instead of back out to sea. The pirate still had no idea who they might be and saw no reason to worry, but something about the activity felt wrong, and it made him uneasy. Instead of waiting for the incoming tide to bring them in toward the bay, the men were rowing hard against the tide to make their way in. Blackbeard tilted his head at this unusual move; most fishermen would wait for the tide and thereby save their energy. Perhaps they would be offloading their catch?

He debated the situation with himself for a while and then decided to move his ship into open waters. In case the King's Navy unexpectedly presented itself, he did not want to be trapped in this small bay. He roused the rest of his men and kicked them until they got themselves up and about. They moved reluctantly and with curses and grumbles, but enough of them finally got moving that they could get the ship underway.

Blackbeard then sent a mostly-sobered-up Willy the Whip ashore in a small boat to begin obtaining the last-minute supplies in the small village before they set sail. He had saved this task until the end in order to get the freshest food possible, for it would have to last them over a long trip.

After Willy shoved off, Blackbeard steered the *Adventure* out of the bay and headed north to make a last minute tactical survey. A short burst of wind caught his jib. and the graceful ship glided slowly around the wide opening and sailed toward the north.

Willy the Whip's head was pounding from drinking so heavily the night before, but he obediently rowed the small boat to the wooden dock at the village of Ocracoke. Here, most people dared not refuse to help the fickle pirate; everyone was afraid of his rash behavior and wanted to be in his good graces.

In this tiny village, Blackbeard was more appreciated than feared: his visits always meant good business for the local traders. The more sedate residents made sure to keep far away from the bay when word got out that his ship was anchored there, for there was sure to be rowdiness of all kinds in the area when Blackbeard and his men were about. That was always a good time to keep your wives and daughters safe at home!

Lies in the Sand

It was early in the day yet, but Willy had a lot to do and his captain had wanted it done quickly, so he needed to get started right after pulling up to the wooden pier. When he heard the crew shouting and saw the ship raising sails and anchor, he was surprised but not startled. His captain never told anyone what he was doing ahead of time. He shrugged, pulled up to the dock and went about his business. Willy knew that Blackbeard needed the supplies he was gathering and would be back to retrieve both him and the goods.

Back out in the Ships Channel, the two small sloops began to slowly make their way toward Ocracoke Island and the *Adventure*. Other than the occasional gust, the wind that morning had been non-existent, so Maynard had his men row slowly at first, but then ordered them to pick up speed. Blackbeard kept a close watch on them with his spyglass. He was becoming wary and ever more suspicious with each passing minute. In addition, he did not recognize this particular type of ship; he felt a strong foreboding unlike any he'd known before; the pirate's fraying nerves triggered his internal alarms.

As he watched them, one of the ships grounded itself on a sandbar in the shallows, which was a commonplace-enough occurrence. Everyone knew that finding one's way out of the sandbars in the shallow water around Ocracoke Island and then out to the Ships Channel and the open sea was a tricky business, for these waters were both dangerous and unpredictable. The ever-changing currents moved the sand around constantly, to the extent that even overnight what had been a channel could close up completely. Before long, the other suspicious sloop grounded itself as well, so now both were stuck. Blackbeard laughed at the sailors but kept watching; still, he reasoned, it could be simply fishermen having a bad day.

In order to get off the sandbar, both small ships began to throw their water casks overboard to lighten their load. *Now* the pirate knew that something was amiss; these extreme measures were only taken in emergency situations when sailors were in either in danger or in a hurry.

He now directed all of his attention in their direction. His gut told him that trouble was ahead!

Onboard the sloops, Maynard had determined that they had to get moving off the sandbars, and being thirsty was to be preferred over being dead. He knew that throwing the water casks overboard might cause suspicion, but he had to do it and so gave the order to both ships. Eventually, Commander Hyde's *Ranger* floated free off the sandbar and began to move in the pirate's direction.

The *Jane,* not far behind and now also free of the sandbar, headed at top rowing speed directly for Blackbeard's ship, the *Adventure*! This was clearly cause for concern! Blackbeard hastily shouted orders to the best of his crew, and summoned all his men to action. The motley crew complied, but with a great deal of protestation.

When the two ships closed within sounding distance of Blackbeard, a shouting match, a war of words began. At first, Blackbeard grabbed his speaking trumpet, boldly lied and loudly declared himself to be 'for King George!' He awaited the reaction from the ships.

He had not long to wait. Maynard then also declared himself – to be *from* King George and then raised the Royal Navy flag, with its unmistakable Union Jack. The pirate's ruse hadn't worked; the battle was now engaged!

Blackbeard, thinking that he had the upper hand over these two unarmed sloops in both men and arms, tried to bargain with him, saying that he would spare both ships if they would let him alone. Maynard replied to the pirate that 'it was him he wanted and he would have him, dead or alive.' Realizing that this was indeed the Royal Navy and some kind of trap, Blackbeard cursed them and pledged to kill them all.

Next, Blackbeard put on his customary fear-inspiring spectacle. He laughed his most evil laugh, called for some wine, and loudly drank damnation to the ships. He boldly declared them to be 'cowardly puppies' and said that he would 'neither give nor take quarter.' But, despite the warning, Lieutenant Maynard and Midshipman Hyde fearlessly came after him with both small ships.

Blackbeard turned and fired cannon broadside into the *Ranger*, killing Commander Hyde and most of his officers on the deck, leaving bloody bodies strewn about and no one in command of the handful of survivors who were struggling to keep the ship afloat. Blackbeard gauged his victory over that ship complete, then seized the helm of his ship himself and headed straight for Maynard's sloop, the *Jane*, to take her down. He could not believe the audacity of these British navy men, to come after him – *Blackbeard* – with only a few men, two small ships and no cannon!

Maynard had managed to get his ship moving and back into open water for the coming battle. Blackbeard turned, hoping to lure and ground this other ship on yet another sandbar so that he could then swing around and finish them both off. Maynard's men, armed with only muskets and swords, fired at Blackbeard's *Adventure* and managed to take down her main sail. In the resulting confusion, whoever was steering Blackbeard's own ship lost his way and then grounded the *Adventure* firmly on a sandbar!

But the pirate was not done yet! As Maynard's ship approached, Blackbeard ordered that his guns strafe the decks of the oncoming sloop without mercy and with all ferocity, which they did with deadly effect, killing several of Maynard's men on deck. Blackbeard now felt the defeat was already in his hands!

Not to be stopped, the *Jane* slowed but continued on toward Blackbeard's grounded ship. The men rowed hard, and with all the momentum they could muster rammed her bow into the *Adventure*. The screeching thud and the tumultuous impact threw most all of them to the decks of their ships. After the collision, Blackbeard, seeing that he had the advantage in numbers, ordered his men to board the Navy ship and take no prisoners! He would show this upstart Navy man who was the King of the Carolinas!

Lies in the Sand

The pirates could then smell the victory and responded by eagerly bounding onto Maynard's ship. A vicious hand-to-hand battle ensued as the pirates jumped the rails and came onboard screaming curses, swords and daggers swinging. They would make quick work of the King's men and get away yet again! Blood and body parts quickly began to cover the deck. Amongst the bodies and debris, men struggled with one another and cutlasses flew along with the curses. The decks became even more slippery with bloody fluids.

But Maynard was a cunning officer, and at this point he gave the signal for a dozen of his best men, who had been hiding belowdecks, to come up and join the fight. Suddenly the odds changed drastically, and Blackbeard's ragged crew found themselves outnumbered. Muskets fired, daggers flew and a bloody battle to the death began!

Blackbeard, although already injured, engaged Maynard in a personal sword fight, blades and curses flying through the air! Lieutenant Maynard broke his sword on Blackbeard's gun box, whereupon the pirate broke the guard of it, damaging the lieutenant's fingers. But the brave, injured navy man managed to jump back, pull out his pistol with his mangled hand and shoot Blackbeard, who even yet refused to yield.

Despite being stabbed and shot, the 'un-killable' pirate was still on his feet! Suddenly Blackbeard felt great searing pain cutting deeply into his neck and shoulder, as he was hit from behind by the broadsword of a Scottish navy man. The infamous pirate fell onto the deck, bleeding and laughing as his lungs gasped for air. When they saw that their leader had fallen, his men gave up the battle.

It was later told that, as he lay dying, Blackbeard said to the Scot who had wielded the broadsword against him, "Well done, Lad." To which the highlander replied, "If it not be well done, then I shall do it better!" and promptly gave a second stroke, which took off the head of the infamous pirate and quieted him once and for all.

Lies in the Sand

Commander Hyde's *Ranger*, which had now pulled up on the far side of Blackbeard's ship, joined the action by boarding the *Adventure* and dealing with the few stragglers left on the pirate ship. Maynard's fresh troops on the *Jane*, together with the remainder of the crew of the *Ranger*, managed to wound or kill most of Blackbeard's men in a swift, fierce battle.

As the battle raged, the locals were running to and from the beach watching the engagement and reporting what they saw. Word quickly spread that *Blackbeard had been killed!* Some of the islanders were ecstatic; others who had profited from his visits were perhaps less happy about the situation. But all were certainly stunned at the news of his defeat: Blackbeard was more than a mere man, he was a legend, one who had always managed to escape!

In less than six minutes, the sounds of clashing swords, gunshot and curses subsided. A quiet hung over the bloody waters, broken only by the cries and moans of the wounded. The famous pirate's ragged, hungover crew had been bested by the trained swordsmen of the King's navy. Blackbeard's head was then hung on a pike of Maynard's ship for all to see. The navy began to tend their wounded, and then to mop up the remains of the bodies and broken ships.

Suddenly, a loud scuffle broke out belowdecks on the *Adventure*, and Maynard's men caught a lone pirate (who had been hidden belowdecks) attempting to set fire to the powder and blow up the ship, together with everything near it. Blackbeard had given the order that if ever he lost a battle, this measure was to be taken. Like many other pirates, he declared that there would be no hangman's noose for him!

The King's men stopped the man just before he was able to light the fuse. Had he succeeded, not only the *Adventure*, but the *Jane* and the *Ranger* together with any remaining survivors, would all have been blown to bits in a massive explosion!

At some far distant future time, someone would add a colorful detail to Lieutenant Maynard's factual, historical account of this exciting battle. The story would be told that after its decapitation, Blackbeard's headless body had immediately jumped off the ship and swam around it three times before finally sinking into the water. Until today, this altogether exciting but unsubstantiated tidbit finds its way into most of the tales about Blackbeard's demise, to the delight of listeners everywhere.

But the true and fearsome sight of the pirate's bloody head on a pike of Maynard's ship would certainly become legend enough! Blackbeard's glassy eyes stared straight ahead as his two beard braids blew around in the wind. Artists would render it and journalists would continue to write about The Battle of Ocracoke Inlet for hundreds of years. The appetite of the public for the tale of Blackbeard the Pirate would seem to never be satisfied!

Blackbeard the Pirate was dead; but his legend had just been born.

Lies in the Sand

Chapter 3

Meanwhile, Willy the Whip heard about what was happening out on the water, and how the battle had gone badly for his captain. He observed dead bodies from both sides being dragged ashore to be buried. Being a cunning young man, he quickly decided to lay low and get lost in the post-battle confusion. He would assess his options later. He hoped and prayed that none of the locals who had seen him would turn him over to the British.

In the confusion of wounded men and battered ships, Willy managed to flee the immediate area. He hid out in the woods on the far side of the island for days as the British mopped up, finishing the job of rounding up and securing for trial the handful of Blackbeard's men who had survived the battle on his ship or had tried to swim to shore and safety.

Word had spread all around the Banks that Blackbeard's ship was heavy with treasure. The Lieutenant ordered the *Adventure* thoroughly searched, but he did not discover any gold, gems or valuables. They had expected to find a priceless booty, but only a small amount of gold dust, a few trinkets and a silver cup proved to be all the plunder they could come up with.

Maynard and his surviving men rafted the three ships together and made repairs to bring them all back to sailing condition. They buried the bodies of the King's twelve men lost in the battle, along with Blackbeard and his eleven dead pirates, in shallow sandy graves on Ocracoke Island.

A fortnight later they got underway and headed for the nearest British port. The small fleet sailed northward, celebrating their victory over one of the most nefarious pirates ever to sail the waters in this part of the world. Lieutenant Robert Maynard's bravery would go down in history: he would be remembered as the brave, cunning British captain who had managed to catch and kill Blackbeard the Pirate.

After foraging to survive for the duration of the navy's stay, Willy eventually found out that the British had left Ocracoke. He quietly made his way back into the village and contacted one of Blackbeard's old friends. Willy agreed to work for the man for only room and board if he'd keep the secret of Willy's ties to Blackbeard. The fellow happily agreed; he wasn't about to refuse a human slave – one with a dangerous secret to hide.

The winter of 1718 passed, and at last a large schooner heading south stopped at Ocracoke. Willy stealthily made his way at night to the docks. Finding the captain in good spirits at a local establishment, he discovered their destination. He convinced the man to give him passage to the Caribbean in exchange for his hard work all the way there.

Late the next night he stole away quietly from his master, got aboard the ship and they pulled out early the following morning. The ex-pirate, Willy the Whip, sailed south and never looked back. He was done with these blighted Colonies, their cold weather, and piracy!

Willy promised himself that if he could only get back to the islands, then he would never again leave the Caribbean and definitely not to sail with a pirate! It had been a tempting job to begin with for a young man looking for excitement and adventure, and it had paid well, but a life of constant fear did not suit him. He had learned his lesson, thanked whatever god had allowed him to escape the battle, and determined to now make his living honestly, as a fisherman.

He jumped ship at Montserrat, an island where he was unknown, abandoning his family on St. Lucia forever. He'd been told that his parents had discovered his association with piracy and would never take him back into the family, so Willy decided that it was time to make a different life for himself as a new man with a new name. He invented a sketchy personal history for his life and started over. He took the name Willy Weaver, married a local girl, settled down and slowly melded into the nearby village population.

None of the locals ever discovered his infamous criminal past; Willy eventually became an upstanding citizen and a successful fisherman. As far as anyone on Montserrat knew, he was just another hard-working sailor struggling to feed his family.

Lies in the Sand

Chapter 4

As the years passed, Willy's fishing business expanded and provided well for his growing family. After fathering several daughters, Willy finally became a father at the age of forty to one son, whom he named Thomas. Thomas followed his father into the fishing business and slowly took over as Willy grew old. In time, Thomas married a local Montserrat girl and had his own family, two sons and six daughters.

When Willy was an old man, one warm sunny day he pulled aside Tom's oldest child (his favorite grandson Samuel) and asked the teenager to take him out fishing. Samuel happily accommodated the old man, as he loved to hear the tales of pirates and bloody battles on the open sea that his grandfather had 'heard when he was young'. They reached their favorite spot and threw over the anchor, relishing the silence and the warm air. As they sat in the boat, Willy put down his clay pipe and said, "Samuel, lad, I have something to tell you. But you must promise to keep it a secret. Can you do that, my boy?" Willy squinted one eye and stared at the young man.

Samuel adjusted the cap on his head, grinned and nodded. "Of course, Grandfather. You know that I will." The old man was getting a tendency to ramble these days, but Samuel loved him enough to listen to all of his stories, although he was certain that most of them were made-up. He settled in for what usually became a long listen. It was a pleasant way to spend an afternoon.

Willy cleared his throat and began. "Samuel my lad, I be deadly serious about this, now. Nobody – not your own Pa or Ma or even your grandmother, God rest her soul, knows what I am about to tell you." He cocked his head to the side.

Lies in the Sand

Samuel's ears pricked up. *A family secret, or just the ramblings of a forgetful old man?* Either way, it would be a good story, he decided, and so he put a serious look on his face and nodded at his grandfather to continue.

Willy got comfortable and leaned one arm on the side of the boat, gazing out into the open water. His thinning hair barely covered the age spots on his head; his once-strong body was now broken down, but the old man's mind was still sharp. "'Twas when I was only a bit older than you that it took place. I was working on a ship – a pirate ship to tell the truth – under the famous captain Blackbeard. We were off the coast of the North Carolina Colony in America about the time when this happened…"

Samuel turned to stare at the wrinkled, white haired man and put up his hand to stop the man. "No, not *Blackbeard the Pirate*, Grandfather? Surely you do not mean to tell me that you sailed with *him*? I thought you always lived on this island!" He felt bad about calling the old man out like that; perhaps senility really had begun to set in. *But sailing with Blackbeard? Nothing could be more unlike the man that he knew as his grandfather!*

Shaking his head slowly, Willy said, "No, Samuel, that is what I told everyone, but 'twas back in 1718 – I'll never forget the year or the month; November it was and it was beginning to grow cold – that Blackbeard himself took me and three other lads ashore in a small boat. The men on the ship called me 'Willy the Whip' because they said I was smart, like the sting of a whip." He laughed long and hard, wheezing a bit toward the end.

Samuel sat speechless and wide-eyed as the old man gathered his breath and continued to talk. "We had a good-sized wooden chest with us in the boat, and when we landed, he told us to carry it and follow him ashore. We walked over some dunes and into a wooded area toting the heavy thing. Then we followed him as he wandered about onshore, seemingly without purpose, looking down, *watching his compass*, of all things! On land!"

The old man shook his head and exhaled heavily. "In time, the man himself stopped at a particular place and pointed down. 'Dig here, lads!' he said, then stepped back and watched us. He would not be satisfied until we had dug down into that pit waist-deep at least. Hard work, that, diggin' a deep hole in sand, you know. Then he had us put the chest in and cover it back up. We drug a few branches about and placed some rocks on the spot to conceal the dig, as he told us to."

"Then he gave us a bottle of rum to share." His grandfather's rheumy eyes lit up as he recalled the details. "We lay about under the shade of some scrubby trees and finished the whole bottle in naught but a few minutes as Blackbeard himself stood on a dune and screamed and laughed like a barmy lunatic!" The old man grinned, flashing what was left of his yellowing teeth.

Samuel had forgotten all about his fishing line and was staring slack-faced at his grinning grandfather. "Grandfather! Are you telling me that you *buried treasure* for Blackbeard the pirate?!"

"Aye, my boy, 'tis exactly what I am telling you," he said, leaning forward, sticking his finger into the boy's face and turning serious. "And this is the part that I want you to know about: I am fairly certain that I was the only survivor of the group of four who dug that hole. The others were killed in the battle when the British attacked Blackbeard's ship at Ocracoke Island, where Blackbeard himself was killed." He grimaced. "'Twas a massacre, that one, I heard, and on both sides…"

"You heard? If you were part of Blackbeard's crew, were you not there?" Samuel asked, looking confused.

Willy shook his head. "No, lad, I had been sent ashore to procure us some supplies that day just before Blackbeard discovered that the British were nearby. I watched him hoist the sails, turn the ship and sail out of the tiny harbor like the Devil himself was after them! I knew not what was happening, but went on about me business as I was sent to do.

Suddenly, I heard the sound of cannon fire coming from the water! Not too long after, word spread around the island that Blackbeard had engaged the British navy, and then I heard that he had been quickly defeated – and killed, along with most of his men! They put his head on a pike of the navy man's ship and hung it there as a trophy!"

"Did you see any of the battle yourself?" Samuel asked.

"No, lad, but I managed to watch from the woods as the mangled bodies were brought ashore... and my three mates were among them," he said, looking troubled. "The three who had helped me bury the chest!"

"What did you do then, Grandfather?" the boy asked, his eyes wide in wonder.

The old man tilted his head and stared at the boy. "Lad, 'twas only one thing I could do – I hid in the woods until them British was good and gone! I nearly starved! Then I made me way back into the village and made a deal with one of Blackbeard's old friends to work for no coin if he gave his word not to turn me in!"

"*You* did that?" the boy squeaked.

"Aye. I did," Willy said. "Well now, don't look as though you've seen a ghost, boy, I too was a young man at one time, you know! But I only stayed there on that wretched island until winter passed and a ship came through that was headed back here to the islands. I signed on to sail for passage and worked my way to this island. I have not left it again, and never will!" He crossed his arms and nodded sharply to emphasize his determination.

"God's knees, Grandfather! And our whole family has believed that you were but a lowly fisherman all your life! Tell me all about what it was like to sail with Blackbeard, please!" The young man leaned forward, then realized that his fishing pole was slipping into the water. He quickly retrieved it and tucked it inside the boat, the fishing all but forgotten. His doubt of Willy's sanity left behind, Samuel eagerly waited for more of the incredible story.

Lies in the Sand

Willy nodded slowly. "These stories must stay between you and me, my boy, because no one else must ever hear what I am about to tell you as long as I live. And even long after that if you want to save the family name and have peace in your own life! Can you swear all of this to me on your grandmother's grave?" He squinted sternly at the young man.

Samuel swallowed. It would be difficult to keep that promise secret, but he would do it. What exciting stories his grandfather must have to tell if this were true! He held up his right hand, palm out. "I do swear, Grandfather. I do." He nodded solemnly.

Willy got comfortable again. "Aye, then, let's get to it. The first thing that I am going to tell you is how to find that treasure box we buried, and if you ever do get leave to go to the coast of North Carolina, you must search for it and find it. 'Twill make you a rich man, lad. That much I can promise you!"

Samuel nodded eagerly. "What was in the treasure box that you buried, Grandfather?"

Willy shrugged. "None of us ever found out exactly…but it must have been valuable beyond reckoning, because I heard Blackbeard whisper to his first mate that his retirement would be a rich one, and it was all tied up with that chest that we buried!" He gave the boy a knowing look. Samuel's eyes grew even larger and he leaned in to catch every word.

Willy said, "First you must find your way to the Outer Banks of the North Carolina colony, but be exceedingly careful of the deadly waters that surround that place – many a good ship and its crew have gone down there!" Samuel nodded obediently. "Make your way there with a captain of good experience," his grandfather admonished.

"To begin with, you must go to the small village of Hatteras. Then you sail north for a bit, stay close to the coast and begin watching your compass. When you see the needle of your compass begin to jump about, you be getting close. Go ashore there and begin to walk.

Lies in the Sand

Whichever direction," he said, waving his arm about, "that makes the compass needle dance, go that way until you come to a place where the needle spins around and around like it's got the devil in it." He twirled his finger around in the air and then pointed straight down. "Dig there. That is where you will find the treasure we buried!" He jabbed his finger into the boy's thigh.

The old man leaned forward. "Now, I do not know all the details because Blackbeard was secretive about such things. But I was slyly watching him out of me eye," he said, pointing to his left eye, "and pretending not to be paying attention. And I be fairly certain that he was watching the compass for direction as we walked. When he stopped at last, I could see that thing was spinning like a top! So, keep your compass close, find the spot and then dig – deep – because the chest was in a hole that was this deep." He held his hand up to about three feet above the floor of the boat.

"Now those sands are always shifting about there in that place, so you may have to dig sideways in a circle until you find it, but I guarantee you my boy that it is there. We piled a few rocks atop the place, but who knows what is there now…" He shrugged and got a distant look on his face. "But you go get it and make yourself a rich man! And say a prayer for your grandfather's soul. I was a wicked man in those days." He hung his head sadly. Willy leaned back against the side of the boat and exhaled loudly. Samuel was speechless, trying to absorb all of this tale of adventure and bounty.

After a long moment, Willy continued the story. "A large part of me believes the blighted thing to be cursed," the old man said, looking very serious. "That is what one of the men said, and I later came to believe its truth. Because the Devil was in Blackbeard for sure, and right after burying it, he was killed and his head parted from his neck! And he was not an easy man to catch or to kill…" He got a faraway look in his eyes.

He cleared his throat and stared at the young man, who was so caught up in the story that he hardly moved. Willy went on, "After we buried it, Blackbeard stood atop a sand hill and screamed bloody murder, waving his arms about like this," he said as he demonstrated, "and then laughing like Satan himself! So, if 'tis true the bloody thing is cursed, and you get some bad luck from it after you find it, get rid of the chest and whatever is in it, you hear me, boy?" He shook his finger in the boy's face. "Because the Devil ain't nothin' to mess with!"

Wide-eyed, Samuel swallowed hard and nodded. "Yes, sir, I swear. And will you tell me some more about what happened then, please?"

"Aye, lad, but as I said, you must not tell a soul or your poor old grandfather could still be hung as a pirate this very day, do you understand?" He tilted his head and gave the boy a threatening look.

Samuel swallowed hard, nodded vigorously and settled in to learn about the life of his grandfather, Willy the Whip, who had lived as a pirate on the high seas with Blackbeard.

"And do not forget what I said about the curse, neither!" Willy said in a deep voice.

It was a day that Samuel Weaver would remember clearly as long as he lived.

Lies in the Sand

Chapter 5

Hatteras Island, summer of 1832

Elijah Weaver stopped walking to wipe the sweat from his brow; he spotted a small tree and managed to find a bit of shade underneath it. The sun was beginning to set over to the west; he was tired, hungry and becoming discouraged. As he sat and rested against the trunk, he silently chided himself. *You know that you're wasting your time, you fool; there's no treasure here, it's just a crazy old family story!*

But Elijah's father Samuel had assured him that his very own grandfather, 'Willy the Whip,' had been one of the men who had buried Blackbeard's treasure and that it was definitely there. Rumors were far and wide that Blackbeard had buried a vast treasure somewhere on the Outer Banks of North Carolina, and treasure hunters were always searching for it. That's why Elijah had hired aboard a ship going to America from the Caribbean: to try to find the legendary treasure, its whereabouts being his family's secret for four generations now!

Elijah had been the only boy born to Samuel and his wife. He had four sisters, but Samuel had told Elijah alone the story of Blackbeard's buried treasure, saying that it was not a story for women's ears. Often Elijah had begged his father for more details, but aside from a few pirate tales, the sketchy information about Hatteras Island, the compass and some kind of awful curse, that was all his father could recall, no more. And Samuel always warned his son that the odds were good that it was only a story, and the whole thing was probably an old man's wanderings of the mind.

At first, Samuel had wanted to go after the treasure himself. But not long after Willy told him the story, the old man died. Then Samuel fell in love, got married, and children began to be born... So, the tale of treasure became more and more like a legend or a myth in his mind, complete with the foul curse to scare a man away.

But even though Samuel's grandfather Willy had sworn him to silence, he had related it to his son Elijah reluctantly one day when they were out fishing and nothing was being caught. The day had reminded him of the time his grandfather had shared the secret with him, and he recalled the amazement he had felt as he'd heard it. Samuel relived those feelings clearly as he related to Elijah the incredible story of the young man's great-grandfather, the pirate, Willy the Whip, who had sailed with Blackbeard.

Samuel cautioned Elijah never to reveal to anyone the secret of the treasure or its location, or the fact that Willy had been a pirate, because the honor of their family name was at stake. He had regretted the telling of it shortly afterward and sternly warned his son about the so-called curse as well, playing up the part the Devil had in the whole thing in order to deter any ideas of going after it that Elijah might get.

But the boy could not forget the story, and it became his obsession. He begged his father for more details whenever they were alone. When a ship finally came through headed to the Colonies, Elijah jumped at the chance to go on his adventure. He would become a rich and famous man! No one need ever know exactly how he had located Blackbeard's treasure; many were seeking it at any given time. He would simply be the lucky one who found it!

Samuel objected strongly to his son leaving to search for the treasure, telling him once more that it was just another of the old man's tall tales, and if it did indeed exist it was surely cursed! That's what he had been telling himself all his life anyway, using it as an excuse not to leave the island or his family. In his mind, the whole thing had become just the rantings of a senile old man. And who was to say that it was not? But Samuel had to reluctantly admit that a small part of him wanted to go along on the boy's adventure, and dig right where his grandfather Willy had told him to. So, he understood his son's passion; had he been younger, he might have gone along.

Elijah had been fascinated by the prospect of treasure and he refused to heed his father Samuel's warnings. He had inherited his great-grandfather's spirit of adventure and was anxious to make a name for himself. Now he was finally of an age that he could work his way there to find out for himself. He shook his father's hand, kissed his mother goodbye and told her that he would come back a rich man. She smiled, patted his cheek and cried, wiping her tears with her apron as he boarded the trading ship bound for the Americas.

It had taken Elijah three years to finally get to this place, Hatteras Island, and now the 'here' he was at was proving to be just one sandy hill after another along the Outer Banks of North Carolina. It was a rough and rugged area to be sure. He'd been camping around here for over a week, trudging endlessly through heavy sand, and was now running low on provisions.

But the prospect of finding Blackbeard's treasure was too tempting to give up. Eiljah was still a young man and he had his dreams; he'd worked hard on those ships to save enough money to get here and then buy a small boat for himself. Now he was going to stay until either he found that blasted box or had disproved the whole crazy story!

The small sailboat that he purchased had brought him here from Manteo, a populated village not too far away. He tried at all cost to avoid any locals who might be on Hatteras Island, so as not to give away his true purpose. He skirted the settlements and life-saving stations, and tried to pass himself off as a lone fisherman.

But now Elijah was tired, disheartened and thinking himself to be the worst kind of fool… After drinking his fill of tepid water from the battered canteen, he wiped his brow once more with the dirty handkerchief, got up and began again to search the area. The only clues that the family legend had given about the location were that the area was north of the village of Hatteras, and that it had some strange properties about it that affected a compass in an odd way.

His father had told him that, if you sailed close enough to the land, your compass would 'go crazy' when it was near the spot where the treasure was buried. What exactly that meant Elijah had no idea, but he figured that he'd know it when he saw it. So far, he'd found nothing by boat and had taken to exploring on foot ashore. He had come this far; he may as well finish the search before giving up altogether and heading for home. At least he'd either discover the treasure or put an end to the legend once and for all!

So, compass in hand, he began again to walk around, marking out a grid as he covered sandy areas that all looked alike to him. The late spring weather was warm; still, the evening wind off the ocean cooled his tropical blood enough to make him long for the balmy breezes of Monserrat. He swatted a few mosquitos and continued his systematic coverage of the area.

Unfortunately, the family legend had not specifically said what the treasure was; evidently the men who buried it had not been given access to the inside of the heavy wooden box. Would it still be here after more than a hundred years? Or was Elijah simply a dreamer on a fool's errand? Only time would tell. He trudged through the loose sand, wondering if he were indeed that simple-minded fool.

Just before dark he noticed his compass flicker a bit, so he stopped dead still. He walked a few steps in four directions, noting which one made the compass's needle act up, and so got his heading. He walked slowly northwest, away from the beach and inland a few hundred paces, making adjustments as he went, according to the reaction of the needle.

Finally, he decided that he had found the exact spot, because his compass was indeed 'going crazy', the needle jittering around as if it were alive! Two steps in either direction slowed down the motion, so he felt sure that this must be the spot. The excited Elijah let out a loud whoop, jumped up and down and then looked around, trying to spot some kind of nearby point of interest to mark this place. But it all looked exactly the same to him.

By this time, it was indeed dark, a moonless night, and he was unable to distinguish anything that stood out from the dreary sameness of the sand, scrub and seagrass. His boat was at least a mile away down the beach; and he knew that if he left now, he'd not be able to find this spot again without wasting another day. What should he do? It was far too dark to begin digging!

So, Elijah lay down right there on the spot. He hunted around for some dead branches and leaves to make a bed, managed to find enough material to get most of his body off the sand, and that is where he slept. No way was he leaving this place until daylight came and he could find a way to clearly mark the location! His stomach growled loudly, as he'd eaten the only bread he'd brought with him much earlier in the day. He sipped on the small amount of water he had left and tried to go to sleep, ignoring the pains in his stomach.

Excitement made his heart race and sleep wouldn't come quickly; he thought of all the ways that he would spend his treasure and how he would make a name for himself. Eventually he dozed off, only to be jerked wide awake by the bone-jarring rumble of a loud boom. Lightning flashed in the distance. He looked up just as the first heavy raindrop hit his face. The thunderstorm quickly became a downpour as the torrential rain drove through his clothing, saturating him down to his skin. A nor'easter was storming ashore!

But Elijah refused to move. Throughout the dark night he lay face-down, using his hat to protect the back of his head and neck and propping his face against his crossed arms to keep from inhaling rainwater. The storm gradually eased its force a bit, but as daylight broke, the rain was still falling steadily and the wind had picked up. He was exhausted and didn't have his heavy digging equipment with him; it was back on the boat. So, he looked around for something – *anything* to designate this spot as special so that he could find it again.

Elijah dragged every broken branch and every scrap of anything that was movable to the spot, piling it high as the rain poured down on him. He was bone-weary and could feel that his strength was failing quickly. Even in his depleted condition, he knew that he had to use what little energy he had left to get back aboard his small sailboat, dry off, eat and rest. The last year had been hard on his young body; starvation and scurvy aboard ships, together with work so hard that he thought it might kill him, had all taken its toll on his health.

He sat down to catch his breath and then got up again, walked straight out toward the beach and stopped at the high tide line. From there he began to pace evenly toward the south, counting his paces as he went. If nothing else, he would have a general idea of the distance and his compass would lead him the rest of the way. It was not a perfect plan, but it was all his fuzzy thinking could come up with at the moment. He stumbled a bit as he walked, feeling hot and weak, but forced himself on and kept walking.

As he trudged along for what felt like miles in the pouring rain, he grew weaker and weaker. At last he spotted his boat, drifting in shallow water, but it looked damaged; it had definitely seen far better days. Even though the sails were down, it had been pushed offshore by the storm surge and had suffered some damage. Nevertheless, it looked to be in one piece and the small cabin would be dry; he could get out of his wet sandy clothes, then eat and rest while the storm abated.

After wading out in the stormy water, he clambered aboard the small boat. A quick looking-over told him that she seemed mostly intact. Elijah managed to fall into his tiny cabin, peel off his clothes and shoes, and wrap himself in a blanket. His body ached all over as he tossed and turned and the pounding in his head grew worse. He reached for bread and water, consumed a small bit of each and then lay there on the floor, falling fast asleep on his mat.

The tide came in; wind and waves rocked his boat, but Elijah was now sick and beyond exhaustion. He wasn't aware of anything until much later, when he opened his eyes, realizing that he'd thrown off his blanket and was burning with fever. He stood weakly, bracing himself against the cabin walls and managed to heat some water for tea as he dressed himself in dry clothes. He poured whiskey into the tea and drank it down quickly, its bitterness stinging his sore throat.

The rain seemed to have slowed, and his boat was now grounded, beached at an odd angle. Elijah sat up, still feverish, holding his pounding head in his hands. *He could not die here! He must not, he'd found the treasure!* His great-grandfather Willy had been here over a century before and buried it, and now it would be his! But first, he must get well and strong again, so he lay back down and instantly fell asleep.

The next time Elijah awoke, he felt that the worst of his fever had passed, but his head and body ached as though he'd taken a beating. How long had he been asleep? He sat up and tried to reason out his situation. How many paces down the beach had he walked? Was it five thousand? More? Less? Was the boat even in the same place that it had been when he'd found it? The tide had come in and gone out and he was now afloat again in the shallow waters. There was no telling where the boat had been when he'd come back aboard after his long walk!

Did he still have an anchor? Had he thrown the anchor overboard in his debilitated state? Elijah was confused, couldn't think straight, and so could not be sure of anything. But he was certain of one thing – he had found the spot and it was near here! The very thought of leaving the small cabin and going out into the rain again made him shiver; he'd have to wait until the storm passed completely.

Late that afternoon he woke up once more and took a little nourishment, but his fever still came and went. A plan of action came to him: unable to go ashore, he would wait until night and using his sextant, he'd determine the latitude of this place if the clouds cleared. Then he'd go back to civilization, get strong again, resupply himself and return.

That night the storm clouds passed enough for him to take a reading to determine his general location; he decided that he would head out for Manteo at daybreak. Elijah hated to leave without the treasure, but it was all he could do for now. He must stay alive, and for that he needed food, rest and care.

Feeling a little stronger the next day, Elijah set sail north for the channel over to the inland waterway. After locating the narrow channel, he then sailed up the Pamlico Sound toward Manteo and hopefully, help. But he knew that he would return to Hatteras, and soon. That fact alone gave him the strength needed to fight his weakness and find his way back to the small fishing village in his severely weakened condition.

When he sailed into the Manteo harbor, he pulled in beside the dock, looked up and as he secured his boat noticed a loud commotion going on ashore. A small crowd of people were hollering and arms were flailing about. Well, he was a sick man and it was not his problem, so he would just avoid the flurry of people and voices. After tying up his boat, he stumbled onto the dock and headed toward town, to the rooming house that he'd used before. He needed a bath and some more rest, and then a hot meal or two to get him back on his feet. In his dazed condition, sleep and food were all he could think about.

As Elijah came ashore, he noticed that whatever it was that had the local folks so stirred up seemed to be spreading. He heard a woman scream and turned to see what was wrong. One man had a pistol and was waving it about, demanding something, but with the pounding in his head Elijah couldn't quite hear what the demands were. Suddenly, the crowd started running and Elijah found himself directly in their path. He barely avoided being knocked down by the rushing bodies. As he turned to flee himself, he heard a loud shot and immediately felt a sharp pain in his side. He fell to the ground. Panicked people ran around him, but no one stopped to help.

He felt the blood draining out of his side, and turned to see the shooter jumping onto a boat and trying to get away. As his vision grew fuzzy, he saw the face of a man who leaned over him and said, "This 'un caught the pistol ball, of all the crazy luck! Somebody help me with him, he's bleedin' bad!"

Elijah felt himself fading as several strong hands lifted him. That was the last thing he remembered before the blackness took him.

Lies in the Sand

Chapter 6

A warm beam of sunlight hit his face and Elijah began to stir. Someone patted his cheek and spoke. "Well, son, it looks like you might make it after all!" a man's voice said. Elijah wondered if his father was truly here, but then remembered that his father was far away. *Am I dead?* he wondered. If he was, then being dead hurt a heck of a lot more than he'd been told! He opened his eyes, and as they adjusted to the light he looked around.

Elijah did not recognize the room he was in, or either of the two strangers around him. A man was leaning over his bed and loading up a small black bag. There was also a woman standing by the door. He felt worse than he'd ever felt in his whole life. He moaned and sputtered, "…what, what did you say?"

"*I said*, you will likely make it, but I did not say 'twould be easy," the man said, stopping to look down at Elijah. "You shall be laid up for a long time and then, well, we will just have to see. That lead shot went clean through your liver and then nicked your spine, and you may or may not have the full use of your legs again. Only time will tell. The infection you had in your lungs is now much better and your fever has subsided, but you are by no means out of danger. You must be one tough so-and-so to have survived this long! By the way, what is your name, son?"

His name? It took a long moment of focus for the answer to come. "Elijah. Weaver. Elijah Weaver. Where am I?" He managed to mutter, his throat as dry as sand.

The man reached for a glass of water, held it up to Elijah's mouth as he drank thirstily, and then stepped back. "You are in the village of Manteo at the house of Frederick Bantam. It was the closest place to where you got shot, and the family has been good enough to take you in for these few days you've been unconscious. You should be grateful for the care you have received here – 'tis not like everybody was eager to take in a shot-up stranger! You are indeed lucky that they are such good people." He snapped his bag shut, stood straight and turned toward the door.

"Wait!" Elijah croaked. "I was... shot? Did you say that I got shot?"

The doctor stopped, turned back and patted Elijah on the arm. "Yes, boy, you were shot by a crazy man with a gun! It could have been any one of us, but you were the unlucky cuss who caught the ball and it took you down! And in my judgement, you were a very sick man *before* you ever got shot!" He looked down with compassion. "'Twas a stroke of the worst of bad luck to be sure, but the good folks of Manteo will take care of you." He gave the young man a warm smile.

Turning to the woman, he added, "I shall be back to check on him tomorrow, Edith. After that, I will send Susan to change his dressing every day. Send for me if his fever returns. Do not let him try to get up and around. You know what I mean..." He raised one eyebrow and gave her a knowing look.

Nodding slightly, she said, "As you say, Doc, we will see to it. Thank you for coming," She showed the doctor out and followed him, closing the door behind them. Elijah drifted off again and was awakened some time later by the same woman. She touched his shoulder and prodded him gently. "Doc said you need to eat something," she said firmly.

Knowing a motherly order when he heard it, Elijah pushed himself up with his arms so she could fluff his pillow, and then she sat beside him on the bed. Holding a spoon to his mouth, she touched his lips. "Open up. This is soup, warm and good. Eat all you can."

He let her spoon in the broth, as if feeding a small child. His mouth watered as he tasted it; it was delicious and the warmth as he swallowed the fishy broth. His dry throat and stomach felt wonderful and his whole body relaxed. "Thank you, Ma'am," he managed to croak. "That is good, truly!"

As she fed him, she talked gently to him. "So, your name be Elijah Weaver, you say? I do not recognize that surname, and you do not seem to be from around here, 'cause nobody here knows you. But it was the worst of luck that you got shot. That crazy fool pulled out a pistol and started waving it around and next thing you know, there you were layin' on the ground!" She sighed sympathetically.

"I...I was shot?" He asked between bites. He thought he had dreamed the whole thing.

"Yep. The other men jumped on the blighter and took him down after he shot you, but the damage was done by then. You are real lucky to be alive, 'twas a wild shot and coulda blowed your brains out." She shook her head sadly. "But it be damage enough, I reckon. And you already had the look of the very sick about you as well. How are you feelin' today?"

He stopped eating long enough to assess his body's condition. "My back and side hurts something awful and I be weak as a newborn babe, but like the doctor said, I am alive and kickin' so I cannot complain, I reckon." He tried to smile.

She tilted her head to the side and Elijah could see the concern in her lined face. "Hmmm... about the kickin' part – can you move your feet or wiggle your toes?" she asked.

"Uh..." Elijah's eyes went wide. "I cannot feel em movin', but I told em to move!" He stared down at his still legs.

She patted his hand. "Do not fret, boy. Doc Baum says 'tis probably temporary, and you will doubtless walk with time. 'Til then, you shall just get around the best you can." She shoveled more soup into his mouth. "The doctor had to cut you wide open to get that lead ball out of your back, so your pain is from that deep cut trying to heal. Doc's daughter Susan is a nurse, and she will see to your day-to-day care. She takes good care of people."

With nothing left to say, Elijah simply ate until the bowl was empty. His mind was not processing the words or the images of him being unable to walk. He closed his eyes tight and fell back against the pillow. Despite the warm food, his stomach churned with anxiety; would he be a cripple for the rest of his life? *No, he could not face a future like that*!

The nice lady patted his shoulder. "You just get some rest, now. My boy Jared will come in later to help you with the… necessary things you might need." She wiped his mouth, and he felt her rise from the bed and move toward the door. She stopped, turned and asked, "Where you be from, boy? You sound like you come from the islands…" He looked up and nodded, and then heard the door close gently as his eyelids dropped down.

Elijah slept on and off for days, coming around sporadically, and finally felt well enough to sit up in bed and look around one sunny afternoon. Susan had come daily to check on his wound and give him soothing words of comfort. But his legs and feet still wouldn't move; he pounded his fist on the mattress in frustration; his eyes began to water. His feeling of helplessness was heated by his anger at being, not only bedridden now, but crippled as well. He took several deep breaths and tried to clear the cobwebs from his head. *Where was he and why was he here?*

Manteo, Manteo, North Carolina, that's where he was! He had come here because of… the treasure, Blackbeard's treasure! He'd found the treasure, but then he got sick or something… He remembered making it back to the dock but after that – nothing. That must have been when he'd been shot. He moaned and pounded the hard-stuffed mattress again with both fists, beating it with what little strength he had.

No, no, not now! Not when he'd finally realized his dream! He couldn't tell anybody about it either, because then they would doubtless go and find the treasure and leave him out of it. Come to think of it, he wasn't sure exactly where he'd found it, he was fuzzy about the details. Perhaps it would come to him after a time…

As his body sought sleep, his mind rolled around the few snatches that he could remember: the compass, the rain, the storm, sleeping in his boat, and finally waking up to make it here, only to get shot. He drifted off once more, hoping that all of this was truly a bad dream and that soon he'd wake up back in his boat.

Lies in the Sand

Chapter 7

As Elijah began to heal, the community took him under their collective wing, agreeing that he was innocent of any wrongdoing and had taken a bullet that could have hit any one of them. One kind man fashioned some crutches for him, and soon he was able to drag himself outside and up and down the dock little by little. Being able to get himself outside to the privy restored a measure of his self-respect.

The local physician, Dr. Baum, had told him that he might or might not get the use of his legs back, and to get up and get around the best he could because he was weak and needed the exercise. He had lost a lot of blood, but his wound was healing nicely thanks to his quick treatment and ongoing care.

Doc Baum's daughter Susan came by to see him almost every day, at first to minister to his medical needs, and after that to simply talk with him. Her kindness touched his heart and she soon became his closest friend. She gave him practical suggestions on how to deal with his new, awkward situation, and she didn't make him feel like less of a man just because he needed crutches to get about.

Soon Elijah became a fixture down on the docks, spending his days talking with the fishermen and the locals. His naturally sunny attitude drew the townsfolk to him. He offered to repair a net for one of them; he'd been on boats for so long that it was second nature to him. Before very long, he was making a little money mending nets and any other fishing supplies which needed repair. At least he still had the use of his hands, and he was getting better and better at this tedious work. He kept alive in his heart the hope of walking again.

The men of the town, who realized that it could have been any one of them who took the bullet that had crippled Elijah, built him a simple shelter down by the water together with a covered place to work, out of the rain and the sun. Susan visited regularly, and she and the other women helped keep him fed. As he mended nets, his thoughts were working out a plan on how to retrieve the treasure once he was walking again. His dream was still very real to him, and he wasn't going to let crutches keep him down for long.

Daily Elijah tried to move his toes, his feet, anything he could. Once in a while he thought that he might see a bit of movement in his left foot, but as soon as that feeling came, it would go away again. Every day he prayed and tried harder and harder to make the effort that would have him walking soon.

After six months, the doctor came to the docks, sat down and talked with him as he worked on nets. "Elijah, you got yourself a rough deal, and everybody knows it." He shook his graying head. "Wrong place, wrong time, as they say. But you are doin' alright for yourself, using what you still got and making a life here on the waterfront." The old man laughed. "Heck, you will probably live longer than the rest of the fishermen! They be out there in all kinds of weather, scratchin' a livin' out of the water, and you be here, takin' care of yourself. You shall do fine, my boy. You will…uh…uh…" the doctor stammered.

Elijah looked up and stopped what he was doing. "What are you tryin' to tell me, Doc? I am still gonna walk, given enough time, right? You said that 'twould take time…"

Doctor Baum looked out toward the water and was silent for a long moment. Without turning his head he said, "Well, 'tis not lookin' good, son. You got no feelin' in that right leg still and the left one be a bit better, but still is weak and unsteady, and cannot begin to support your weight." He turned toward Elijah. "By this time, if the legs would be getting better, we should be seein' more than that. So, it might be good to get your mind settled on the thought that you will be needing those crutches from now on." He nodded toward the crutches laid at

Lies in the Sand

Elijah's side. He looked at the younger man with compassion and sadness in his eyes. "I am sorry, Elijah, truly I am."

Elijah went back to working on the net with determination. "I shall walk again, I will run again, Doc, you shall see. Do not give up on me just yet. I have got important stuff to do."

The doctor reached over and laid his hand on Elijah's arm; the young man's spirit was admirable. "Just remember this: you have to work with what you got now, not with what you hope to have. You are doin' a good job of that so far, and you still be young and healthy. You are the kind of man who will do the best he can and you shall accomplish amazing things, I am certain."

Elijah looked out to sea. "Work with what I have got, say you? Well, that is what I shall do, and someday what I have got will surprise everyone." He turned to look at the doctor. "I have got amazing things to do, that is for sure. And I am going to do 'em!"

The doctor removed his hand from the boy's arm and stood up. "I believe you, Elijah. I do. If any fellow be man enough, it would be you."

Elijah made a face. "And, Doc, about that part… about me manhood and all… I need to ask you a question…" he began. "Uh…uh…"

"Well, spit it out, then, lad."

"Will I ever be able to, uh, father children, do you think?" He couldn't look directly at the older man as he asked his question.

Doc slapped him on the shoulder. "That's another thing that time will tell about, son." He added, "Your man-parts be working, are they?"

Elijah nodded. "Aye, seem to be about their business as usual."

Doctor Baum laughed. "Well, if it be children you're after, then first you got to find yourself a wife. Do not want to be puttin' the cart before the horse, now do we!" He snorted.

Lies in the Sand

Elijah looked up, pleased with the doctor's answer. "About that, sir, I was thinking about asking your daughter Susan if she might be so inclined…" he said hopefully. "Would you be objectin' to that – I mean me asking her – and if she says yes…"

The doctor sat back down. "Susan? Hmmm. Well, she does seem to think highly of you." He looked him straight in the face. "The girl doubtless has a heart of gold and she is the hardest workin' woman I know, but Susan's got a face as plain as truth and a figure like a fence post, bless her heart. You be sure about this?" The old man was torn between his plain daughter's chance for happiness and the problems she would be buying for herself by taking up with this one.

Elijah grinned. "I ain't exactly the catch of the day, myself, Doc. But I dearly love the girl and will do my dead level best to take care of her, and I believe that she would do the same for me. You cannot ask for much more than that, can you?"

The doctor thought for a long moment and shook then his head. "No, Elijah, that is about all you can hope for in this world in a mate. Her mother was the light of my life, and there has never been another woman for me since she died." He reached over and put his hand on Elijah's shoulder. "If Susan goes along with this idea of yours, then you have my blessing, son! And I shall expect those grandchildren you spoke of!"

A wide grin covered Elijah's face. His future was now going to be his family. And he'd walk eventually, he was sure. He would find his treasure and be a rich man!

Susan agreed right away and the two of them married and lived with her father. Two years later she gave birth to their only child, a bright and happy little girl they named Lilly. Elijah learned to get around well on his crutches, and with the doctor's help – and the hard work of his wife and daughter – he managed to build himself a solid business selling supplies to the locals.

Lies in the Sand

While the memory of the treasure still haunted him, Elijah had at last made peace with the fact that he would never recover it. As a disabled man, he would hardly be able to recover it on his own, even with his best effort, and he decided not to share the secret with anyone, not even Susan.

The haunting possibility of the so-called curse connected with the treasure had become very real in his mind, and he refused to chalk his run of bad luck up to coincidence or chance. If seeking the treasure had crippled him, then he would stay far away from it. He would be happy with his work, his small family, and continue to do as his father-in-law had advised, to 'work with what he had.'

Lies in the Sand

Chapter 8

37 years later, 1880, Manteo, North Carolina

The two young men stood shoulder to shoulder, silently looking down into the deep hole long after everyone else had left. Their tears had dried, but they simply could not bring themselves to leave the graveside of the man who had raised them as his own.

A roughly dressed fellow nearby cleared his throat and leaned on his spade. "Boys, your grandpa Elijah was as fine a man as ever lived, but I need to get this here grave closed up and finished before dark…"

Taylor and Thomas Jennings looked up at the man and nodded. Taylor, the older of the twins by a few minutes, took his new position as family head seriously and he answered for them both. "Then you better get to it, Jed. And our thanks to you for everything you have done."

"It is what I do," Jed replied, shrugging and lifting his shovel.

As the first shovelful of dirt hit the pine box, Thomas elbowed his brother. "I cannot believe the old man's gone, he seemed so tough… Even though he was crippled, he was as strong as an ox and as good a man as any…" He cleared his throat and looked up at last. "Well, let us get ourselves back home, I suppose that folks will be worried."

Taylor nodded and they turned as one and headed toward the dirt road that led back home. From behind, and many said that from in front, the two of them could not be told apart. Their grandmother Susan had been able to do so, but over the years the twin boys had played that game with everyone else on the island at one time or another. They walked in silence, hands clasped behind their backs, for most of the mile or so. Then Taylor stopped and said, "Tom, now we are all that's left of the family, you know."

Thomas nodded. "Not that there was ever a lot of us to begin with," his brother said. "Most folks got big families, but Mamma was an only child, and Granny Susan was an only child as well. Grandpa Elijah never talked about his family much, except to say that he'd left them all behind in the islands. Grandpa Doc moved here from somewhere in Virginia as a young man, and I don't know if we ever met any of his people. So, I reckon it is just us." He shook his head.

Their mother Lilly had died from complications of their difficult childbirth. Their father left the island shortly thereafter, never to be seen again, so Elijah and Susan had raised the boys as their own. The two of them became their grandfather's legs and their grandmother's babies to comfort her after the loss of her daughter Lilly, her only child and the twin's mother.

Taylor went on. "But then, we have got the mercantile and the fishing supply business, a sturdy home and some property, so we shall not have to worry. We just need to work hard and we will be alright, brother," he added.

Thomas nodded. "'Tis true, we have been pretty much runnin' the place since Grandpa Elijah got sick last year. But if we are going to get ahead, we need to get us some wives and have younguns of our own to help us out," Tom said matter-of-factly. He added, "Yes, we will continue the family name. And that makes us the keeper of the family secret as well."

Taylor had been walking but stopped short when he heard that. "What – do you mean Grandpa Elijah's tall tale about Blackbeard's 'cursed' treasure down by Hatteras?" he scoffed. "You know that was nothing but the ramblings of a crippled old man!" Taylor had never taken it seriously and had made light of it whenever it was mentioned by their grandfather.

Thomas shook his head. "But what if it is true, Tay? What if it is really there? Remember the time Grandpa Elijah got us all a ride on that boat that delivers supplies to the Life Saving Stations? He pointed out the general area and told us the whole story again, how his grandfather had told it to him, and said that he had actually found the location of the treasure!"

Taylor rolled his eyes in disbelief. "Yes, and he swore us to secrecy, I know. Look, Tom, he was a fine old man, but by his own admission he had been sick out of his head when he made it to Manteo, and then he got shot and, well, you can't take all that nonsense about a buried treasure seriously, can you?" He shook his head in disbelief. "*Blackbeard the Pirate*? No doubt he was seeing things in his fevers and imagined the whole business!"

Thomas shrugged. "Well, I do wonder from time to time…. It couldn't hurt to look for it, could it?"

Taylor laughed. "Very well then, you get your compass and head out, go up and down Hat'tras Island lookin' for a place where the thing goes crazy. Let me know how that all works out," he said, pushing the idea away with his hands and his mind. "I have got a future to build right here on Roanoke Island, in Manteo. This place is growing fast, and we are going to be important men here someday, brother. Now, let us go and eat some of that good food waiting for us back at the house!" The two of them started walking again.

Thomas smiled. "And look at some of those pretty girls that will be there to give us some fine sympathy!"

Taylor grinned. "Yep, now you got the idea! That's our future, Tom, not some crazy old family legend!"

"Well, I am going to get down there someday, Tay. I mean it. If there's a treasure down there, it's our family duty to find it!"

Taylor punched his brother in the arm. "Don't be foolish, Tom! The only treasure for you and me is right here on Roanoke Island, and we'd better get to building it now before it slips away from us!"

Thomas stopped walking, turned to look at his twin and said, "Well, as you say then, I will focus on building our business, but I am not giving up on that dream of Blackbeard's treasure. Someday, I am going to look for it, I care not what you say!"

Lies in the Sand

Taylor laughed out loud. "Whatever pleases you, brother. But for now, let us become the important men that we were meant to become. Come along, folks are waiting for us, including some very pretty girls who want to marry important men like us!" He pulled Thomas by the arm. "And I know which one of them you want!" He elbowed his brother.

Thomas, silent and thoughtful, begrudgingly followed his twin. If it was up to him, and it looked like it was, then he would be the one to uncover the family secret at some time in the future. Blackbeard's cursed, buried treasure would have to wait for him to dig it up...

Chapter 9

1922, Manteo, NC

Thirty-two years later

The two men walked slowly through the woods toward home as they continued their serious conversation. The younger one stopped. "Father, I don't believe it, I just cannot believe it," Alfred said, putting his hands on his hips. "It sounds like some kind of pipe dream!"

Thomas put his arm on the younger man's shoulder. These days his son Alfred was taller than him. He was a good boy, a hard worker, and the favorite of Thomas's twelve children.

"I know it sounds hard to believe, Son. And really, the whole of the story is lost in our family history. But my grandfather passed down the secret to me and your uncle Taylor, just like his grandfather passed it down to him. Your great-great grandpa Elijah Weaver actually *found* the treasure, but then he got sick, and then he got shot, and after that he was unable to get back to find it again. And even though Grandather told me that it was probably cursed, he told me where to look, and I am determined to go there before I leave this earth. Do you want to go with me or not?" He looked into the young man's eyes.

Alfred took off his hat, wiped the back of his hand across his sweaty brow, and put his hat back on. "Look, Father, I want to believe you, I really do, but it's just that… well, *Blackbeard the pirate*? That was over two hundred years ago! It's probably just a lot of hogwash, like all the rest of these fishermen's tales."

Lies in the Sand

Thomas sat down on a nearby fallen log, laid his walking stick to one side, and patted the place beside him. Alfred obediently sat down. "Alright, then, let us say that it *is* just an old family legend. You know, those legends all start somewhere, from something that actually happened. If this one is true, then we have a treasure to find! If it's just a bunch of hooey, as you say, then all we have wasted is a day of our lives. And I for one have wasted a lot more time that that!" He crossed his arms emphatically.

The younger man sat silently as he thought about it. He dearly loved his father and wanted to please him, and if a day spent on a boat would make him happy, then that's what he would do. The old man was getting up in years and had a bad heart, the doctor said. He might not have that much time left, so Alfred would do what he could to make him happy in the years he had remaining.

"But what about the so-called curse that comes along with the treasure? Don't that scare you a bit? It does me!" Alfred said.

Thomas shook his head slowly. "Nah. It's just superstitious gibberish, boy! There ain't no curse on that wooden box! Just 'cause Blackbeard died and Grandpa Elijah got crippled – that don't mean the treasure's cursed!"

Alfred removed his cap and wiped his forehead with his arm, then held the cap in his hands, twisting it. Finally, he looked into the old man's rheumy eyes. "Alright, Father, as you say. I shall take you. I will get hold of a boat for us and the two of us will make it down there. How does next week sound to you?"

Thomas perked up. "That'd be mighty fine, Son! It's been a lifelong dream of mine, you know, but my brother Taylor worked me so hard in the mercantile that I never had a chance to get down there. And then me and your Ma had so many kids that I never had the time. Plus, she was a hard taskmaster, your mother." He laughed, and then sighed. "But now, with both of them gone, well, I don't see no reason not to go…"

Alfred reached over and patted his father's shoulder. "Okay, then, Father. Next week we shall go on your adventure!"

Lies in the Sand

The old man looked into his eyes and Alfred would have sworn that he saw a tear there before Thomas turned away. He cleared his throat and said, "Good enough, son. Good enough."

Lies in the Sand

Chapter 10

The following week

Off the coast of Hatteras Island

"You got to get us in closer to shore, Alfred!" The old man called out, holding his compass up and waving it around anxiously.

"I'm trying, Father, but it's rough surf today!" The younger man answered, struggling with the tiller on the small motorboat. "I don't want to wreck us on a sandbar!"

"It must be the curse," his father muttered, shaking his head.

"I thought you said that the curse was just gibberish!" Alfred said, still fighting the tiller.

"Well, I wasn't going to mention it again, but…my grandfather Elijah did seem to believe that the treasure was truly cursed. It was what caused him to get sick and crippled, he said. But I never took it serious much before…"

Alfred shook his head and exhaled loudly. *Crazy old man, why did I ever agree to do this?* "How much longer before we can turn back?" he asked, as the rough waves tossed them about.

"Let's go a little farther south, please. See that point there? Let's make it that far before we call it a day," Thomas said, pointing to a sandy outcropping.

Finally! Alfred steered the boat toward the point, giving the small engine as much gas as he dared.

Lies in the Sand

"Wait, stop! Stop here!" Thomas called out suddenly.

Alfred jerked his head around. "Here? Why?"

"Because my compass is acting funny! Get us in closer, quick now!"

Alfred cut the engine to an idle, turned the boat toward shore and asked, "Do you want to beach her here?"

Thomas waved his compass around in the air. "A little further south, just a little more!" Alfred obediently increased the gas and the boat began to move slowly. "There! Now, take us in!" the older man shouted.

Alfred fought the heavy surf and managed to make it to the beach. "Father, this is crazy! There's nothing here but the same old thing we've been passing all morning! Sand and more sand!" He jumped out of the boat and began to pull it ashore.

Thomas crawled out of the boat and stumbled onto the sand. He was breathing hard. "But look," he said, pulling his frail body upright, "look at my compass!"

Alfred reluctantly humored the old man and studied the compass. It actually was acting strangely, the needle fluctuating far too much! He scratched his head, took it from his grandfather and began walking toward the land. He could almost feel it vibrate as the needle jumped around.

"It really is going crazy, you're right, Father," he said, taking off toward the undergrowth. "Maybe there's something to this, after all…" He looked back at the old man trying to slog through the heavy sand. "You stay here and I'll look around. Walking through this heavy sand with that stick of yours will be too hard for you."

Thomas reluctantly agreed, but refused to sit down, leaning on his cane instead. As Alfred walked inland, he noticed that as he drifted south, the compass calmed down, but if he headed northwest, it seemed to come to life. He climbed quickly over the dunes and came to a point where the needle fairly flew around, as if North were a direction that did not exist.

Lies in the Sand

"Father, come look!" Alfred called out. He marked the spot where he stood and waited for his father to come to him. "Papa, come on!" He yelled. There was no sound coming from the beach, but then the surf was loud and the old man's hearing was going. His father wouldn't answer his calls if he hadn't heard them; and he was probably too weak to climb over the sandy rise anyway. So, Alfred dragged a large piece of driftwood there to mark the spot and went back to look for his father.

As he topped the dune, he saw Thomas lying in the sand. Alfred ran to him, calling out as he went. "Papa, Papa!" When he reached the old man, his father was face down in the sand. Gently turning him over, he yelled, "Papa, please, talk to me!" He gently brushed the sand off Thomas' face.

The old weathered eyes fluttered open and seemed to focus on the young man. Thomas smiled. "You found it, didn't you, boy?" he asked weakly.

"Yes, Father, I found the place where the compass goes crazy! I marked it, too, so we can find it again when we come back..."

Thomas shook his head slowly and spoke with great effort. "No, do not come back, Son! This place is truly cursed, it must be... Better to just leave it be and go on with your life. I was a crazy old coot for wanting to come here; my grandfather warned me, and I'm warning you – don't come back! Just leave it alone and let time take care of it." He grabbed his chest and winced. "No treasure is worth this...". Thomas closed his eyes and breathed out heavily. Alfred could almost see the life draining out of him.

Although Alfred waited for him to take another breath, it didn't come; he shook the old man. "No! No, Papa, no!" He clung to his father, crying and screaming, until the body went completely limp in his arms. Alfred looked up and cried aloud, "*Why?* Why take him now? Just when his dream had come true?" He wept for a long time and then rose, looking first inland, and then out toward the sea as he battled with his emotions. His brothers and sisters would be heartbroken and probably blame him for taking him out on the boat at his age. But mostly, he would miss this dear old man who had been there for all of his children for as long as he could remember, loving and teaching them.

Lies in the Sand

Gently, he lifted the frail body and placed it in the boat. A wicked-looking storm was heading their way, and he'd have to hurry. He thought about where to go, what to do, and decided that this place of Blackbeard's treasure must indeed be cursed. *I will never return here! And I will never mention it to another human being!* The secret and the curse would die with him. He headed the boat back toward Manteo, fighting his tears as well as the angry sea.

Chapter 11

As the years passed, Alfred thought more and more about the day his father Thomas had died. The lure of Blackbeard's treasure beckoned, but he was afraid to go there himself. The pain of losing his father, together with his own superstitiousness about that day and that place, had prevented him from going back. He rationalized that his father had been a sick old man with a weak heart; the excitement alone had probably killed him. And yet, a part of him wanted to know despite his fear.

But at the same time he didn't want anyone else to have the property; it was his legacy, the legacy of his family secret. So, when the old fisherman who owned that stretch of beach passed away, Alfred made a deal to buy several acres around the piece of land where his father had died, but he told no one.

Alfred himself had no children, so he put the deed to the Hatteras Island property away safely, along with a letter explaining the treasure and the curse. If his favorite little sister Iris ever had children, he'd pass the property and the legend on to a nephew. Perhaps by then there would be a safe way to locate this so called 'treasure'. If not, well then, land was always a good investment, even out on that blasted island... *but what crazy fool would ever want to live way out there?*

Alfred's sister Iris gave did birth to one son in 1935, William, and one daughter, Sally, two years later. Sally married and moved to Raleigh in 1958. Her son William received a large pile of legal documents upon his Uncle Alfred's death. His dear uncle had bequeathed property and money to him, but William had been so overcome by grief that he simply could not plow through all the paperwork. So, when he was sent to Vietnam as a soldier in 1964, he set it all aside to deal with at a later time.

Lies in the Sand

After his return from two tours of duty in that jungle hellhole, William came home a changed man, deeply scarred physically and emotionally. He avoided people for the most part and threw himself into his work at the Norfolk ship yards. He drank heavily and never married.

William's sister Sally hardly ever heard from him and had to call him every few years to make sure that he was alright. She worried about him, but had her hands full with her husband and her new career.

She had given up on having children when her son, Felix, was born in 1978. Felix was lavished with attention from the day of his birth. Sally's husband divorced her when Felix was only five years old. She died in 2015 a selfish, bitter woman, traits she passed on to her only child.

By the time Sally's troubled brother William died in 2017, the man had become a wealthy recluse. His nephew Felix didn't know and didn't care.

Lies in the Sand

Lies in the Sand

Part Two

Lies

of the

Present

Lies in the Sand

Chapter 12

Present day, Norfolk, Virginia

"Is this a prank call?" The young man demanded. "If you're trying to scam me, man, you're going to be sorry you ever messed with –"

"No, sir! I assure you this call is deadly serious and has to do with the estate of your great uncle, William Sanders, who died a few months ago. Please hear me out, Mr. Benefield. If you are the Felix Benefield we're looking for, this is important news for you," the caller pleaded.

"I don't know whether to hang up on you or not, so I'll give you just thirty seconds to get to the point," Felix spat. He was an impatient, paranoid skeptic who assumed everyone was out to get him.

The man on the other end cleared his throat. "Right. Okay, this is how it all came about: your great-uncle William died last November. His estate was a complicated one, his holdings complex, and it took some time to locate his will. He had no children, and it turns out that he left most of his assets to various charities or a few select individuals. By the time we got it all sorted out, we realized that one particular asset, a deed to some land out on the Outer Banks, was designated to go to his nearest living male relative. It took us a while to track you down – you do move around a lot you know – Mr. Benefield, but you are that relative!"

Felix sat down in a nearby chair. He did vaguely remember his mother mentioning her Uncle Willy, but their family had never been close; he was an only child and his parents had split up when he was just a baby. And he *had* been out of the country a lot in the last year. So, he began to see that, realistically, this could be true, but… "Okay, then let me ask you this, Mr. … uh, what did you say your name was again?"

"I am Frank Dalman with the firm, Steed, Dalman and Browning in Raleigh, North Carolina. Google us if you don't believe me," the man said tartly, quickly tiring of dealing with this abrasive person. Most people were happy to hear that they'd inherited something, but this smart-alec seemed to want to challenge him at every turn.

"Okay, then," Felix said. "If what you say is true, then tell me the name of my mother, Uncle William's niece." He waited while he heard papers being shuffled around.

The attorney replied, "Here it is. Her name was Sally Benefield, maiden name: Morton. I see here that she passed away a few years ago. My condolences on the loss of your mother as well as your great-uncle. *Now* do you believe me?" Mr. Dalman asked, irritation clearly evident in his tone of voice.

Felix nodded even though the attorney had no way to see that. "So, then... what was it exactly that good old Uncle William left me again?" he asked.

"It's a deed to a piece of land that borders the National Seashore property on Hatteras Island, out on the Outer Banks. Are you familiar with that area?"

Felix tried to recall some facts about her family that his mother had shared with him. If he'd been paying attention at that time it would have been easier. "Well, I believe some of my mother's family came from there, now that you mention it. Somewhere on the Outer Banks, I'm not certain just where." He paused for a moment. "Say, is this property that he left to me valuable?"

The attorney laughed. "*All* property on the Outer Banks is valuable, son, it's just a matter of location that determines its actual worth. I believe that this section is beachfront, and that makes it prime real estate for beach houses, if I'm not mistaken."

Felix's eyes grew large. "Beach houses! Wow, that sounds like big money! Alright, then, how do I go about making this business legal so that I can sell that property?"

Lies in the Sand

The lawyer exhaled deeply. He found it a pity that most people tended to value their dear departed relatives on a cash-only basis. "Come to Raleigh at your earliest convenience and we'll get it all settled for you – minus any fees, of course."

"Of course," Felix answered sarcastically. "Hey, this is almost as good as winning the lottery! I haven't had a turn of good luck like this in a long time, and I'm due for one!"

Mr. Dalman cleared his throat. "There's just one more thing, though; trivial, but worth mentioning. The deed comes along with an old, undated letter that is to be passed down to each owner of the property, and it's an... odd letter. Something about a family curse. Probably nothing, just old superstition, but I thought I'd mention it."

"A curse? All the more reason to sell it quickly!" Felix said, laughing. "That'll make the curse somebody else's problem, not mine!"

The attorney rolled his eyes, said goodbye, hung up and moved on to his next phone call. *Not even a thank you...* This was one inheritance case that he'd be glad to be rid of.

Lies in the Sand

Chapter 13

Hatteras Island, the Outer Banks of North Carolina

Present day

"Hey, look, Annie, there's going to be an auction of some land nearby," Terry said to her friend. "It's right here in the paper." She jabbed the newspaper with her finger. "Right here!"

Annie looked up from her ipad. "You still read the newspaper!" she said, grinning. "I thought nobody under forty did that anymore."

Terry gave her the evil eye. "Hey, I was born and raised on this island and a lot of the stuff that happens 'round here doesn't make it to the online sites! I like to keep up," she said, lifting her chin and turning back to study the local paper. "Hmmm... I believe that this property that's up for auction might be very near here. They say it's the first four lots south of the National Seashore."

Annie looked up, startled. "That can't be!" She dropped the tablet and pointed straight down. "This place here is the first private property south of the National Seashore. Let me see that!" she said, grabbing the paper from Terry. "No...no, it can't be..." Annie stammered as she read. "My father assured me that the value of this property is so high because it is *the* parcel adjacent to the government-owned property. He said that back when the Park Department started buying up private land in the 50's to form the National Seashore, nobody claimed to own anything north of our piece of land." She sat down and read the rest of the article. "I'd better call and find out more about this, because something's fishy somewhere."

Terry made a face. "If this is right, it means that your *Sandy Bottom Bed and Breakfast* might not be the special place that you've been advertising it to be for all this time!" She got a sick look on her face. "And they could even put up one of those stupid mega-gift shops or something like that right next door!"

Annie rubbed her face. "I'm calling my lawyer." Suddenly her busy but pleasant life had grown much more complicated. She reached for her phone.

Two hours later Annie plopped down on a comfortable sofa in the main sitting room of her B&B. She looked around slowly. She'd spent all of her inheritance, plus some borrowed funds, to fix this place up, making it one of the most desirable places to stay on this end of Hatteras Island. And now, if they built up some... some... ugly God-knows-what next door, it could ruin her hard-won reputation for a natural setting, or at least discourage the better customers.

She advertised her B&B as 'adjacent to the wildness and serenity of the National Seashore on Hatteras Island', and her guests loved the privacy that allowed them to roam the beach in that direction, unhindered by visitors from nearby hotels or large private homes.

She had to go to the auction. She had to bid. It would mean putting up her property as collateral, the improvement loans just recently paid off, and then being able to build nothing on those lots next door. But then she thought, *perhaps a nice firepit and gazebo, an extension of the theme of her place.* Well, it couldn't be helped. She had to try to get her hands on that property.

Chapter 14

Felix Benefield signed all the paperwork and then handed over the sale of his Outer Banks property to an auction house in Raleigh, eager to get his money and be done with the whole thing. He was a wanderer by nature, and hoped that this big windfall would finance his travels around the world for quite some time to come. In fact, he'd already decided that he wanted to go to Africa next. He began to call the auction house several times a week to see how long it would be before he got his money.

Patience was not Felix's strong suit; but then he was selfish, immature and known by the few friends he had to have almost no strong suits. His mother had pampered him and denied him nothing, producing a grown man with the temperament of a child.

Ron Bentley, the owner of the auction company, decided to send a representative to photograph and size up the property before the auction took place, in order to placate this irritating man. They would create an attractive website and brochure for the sale. It was a large, unique piece of land and no doubt would fetch a great price.

Daniel Marcus, the appraiser and Ron's right-hand-man, rolled down his window as he made his way south on NC Highway 168 toward Hatteras. This had been a pleasant drive over from Raleigh. It was early spring, the tourist traffic was light, and the weather was beautiful today. He began to sing with the music he was playing. This would be his first trip to the Outer Banks and he was already impressed.

He'd gone online and discovered a bed and breakfast which was located near, in fact right next to, the property to be auctioned. He made reservations for a week and arrived on a Thursday, thinking that would be more than enough time to evaluate the land and even give him a few days off. After all, this was the beach!

Annie had put her property dilemma into the hands of her lawyer, and was trying not to worry about it, because she knew that these legal matters can drag on and on endlessly. But she couldn't seem to get it off her mind because her future was riding on the outcome.

Today she was all set to welcome a few new guests to her B&B, and to make them feel at home during their stay. Their rooms had been aired, flowers had been put on the tables, and she had soft music playing in the background in the sitting areas. The first guest, a single out of Raleigh, was checking in after 2 pm. He was here on some kind of business, he said; that was unusual as most folks came down on vacation. She put him upstairs in Room Four, the only one without a direct ocean view.

She heard a car pull up and peeked out through the curtains in front. That must be him. As he got out of his car, she noticed that he looked fairly clean cut, seemed to be youngish (but no kid, that was good) and was dressed well. She nodded as she sized him up. Her clientele liked to have a certain caliber of guest to associate with, if they did decide to have breakfast or drinks in the evening with the others staying there. This fellow looked alright.

She opened the door as he walked up onto the porch. "Mr. Marcus?"

He nodded, looking at the porch as he took the steps two at a time with his long legs. White rockers and swings with colorful cushions gave visitors a most inviting welcome. It was a relaxing place. He smiled. "That would be me." He put his bag down and reached out to shake her hand. "Are you the lady I spoke with on the phone?"

She gave him a warm smile. "Yes, that was me. I'm Annie Evans, the owner of the *Sandy Bottom Bed and Breakfast*. Glad to have you here! I hope that you'll find everything to your liking."

Daniel stopped sizing up the house and began to notice the woman standing in front of him. Early thirties, he guessed, beautiful eyes, tons of dark hair and a smile that lit up the whole place. He grinned. "You're a bit young to be the owner, aren't' you?"

Lies in the Sand

Normally, that personal comment about her age could have offended her, but coming from him – well, she kind of liked it. He was tall, athletic and his smile seemed to spread all over his face. She was drawn to him immediately. She grinned. "If you're trying to flatter me, it's working, but yes, I'm the owner. My parents built this house in the 70's and left it to me. I moved here five years ago, converted it to a B&B, and have been working hard to build up my business ever since. Do come in and let me show you around, Mr. Marcus." She smiled at him with her best 'hostess' smile.

"Call me Daniel, please…"

"Fine. Then you'll call me Annie." She motioned him inside. "You can put your bag down right there while I show you around. Come on in through here."

He noticed a desk in the sunny foyer, then followed her down a long, spacious hall into a very large room with windows all around. The view of the beach from there was stunning. A few tables and several conversation areas of chairs sat throughout the room, one group facing a large fireplace. Through the many windows and large double doors, he could see a huge screened-in porch overlooking the ocean. "Wow! This place is… well, it's beautiful!"

She smiled. "Thank you for saying so! I'm quite proud of it. My guests all tell me that they enjoy their stay here, and I hope that you will too, Daniel. Come this way." Annie showed him the layout of the common areas, the dining area off to one side, and the grand stairway that led up to the bedrooms. "I only have four units. Keeping it small works well for me. Your room faces the front, and the way the land curves around, you don't have an ocean view, sorry. But there's a lovely view of the Pamlico Sound from your front window, and out the side of your north-facing window you can see the National Seashore."

He looked around, taking it all in and nodding.

She went on. "Breakfast is from eight 'til nine, and there'll be a menu in your room the night before so you can see what we're serving. You indicated on the phone that you have no food allergies, correct?"

He nodded. "Yep. Mamma always said I'd eat anything and sure enough, that seems to be the case," he said, grinning.

Annie was beginning to like the look of that grin. She cleared her throat. "Great. Come along, I'll show you the rest of the downstairs and then take you up to your room." They walked through the large kitchen, then back across the hall, where she pointed out her private area and office and a downstairs half-bath on the opposite side from the kitchen.

The house had been renovated perfectly to serve as an inn, he noticed. The front entrance, small but welcoming, served as a place to check in and take care of business, and the spacious hallway led visitors to the main living area. That large, bright multipurpose room contained the staircase, served as living room, dining area and a gathering place where visitors could chat, read or just hang out. And the three walls of windows displayed the beautiful dunes and impressive Atlantic Ocean beach below – the real draw for the *Sandy Bottom Bed and Breakfast*!

After his tour, Annie showed Daniel up to his room and left him to get settled. She went back downstairs and busied herself with preparations for the next arrivals, but found herself smiling as she thought of the man in Room Four. *Now, don't let yourself get to thinking like that*, she chided herself. *Handsome men come and go, and just because he's here alone doesn't mean that he's not married or otherwise taken. Besides, that's the last thing you need to be thinking about right now!* Her most recent boyfriend had let her down in a big way and she was determined to remain an independent woman after she'd finally gotten rid of 'The Loser,' as Terry referred to him.

Annie had been married for a short time after college, but they'd both been young and hadn't given the relationship time to develop before they made the plunge into a commitment. She had thought of getting married again, but next time she would get to know the man and determine if she could live with him – his good points and his weak points – before she made the decision to marry. Her parents had set a good example as a couple who worked through the problems that life threw at them, and she was determined to make her next marriage last 'til death do us part'.

Lies in the Sand

A short while later, Daniel made his way downstairs to the common area and then out to the back porch. A cool but gentle breeze met him, and he was glad that he'd put on that sweatshirt. It was still too early to even think of going into the ocean, he supposed. He made himself comfortable, spreading out the maps he'd brought along on the large outdoor table. Annie stuck her head out the door and said hello.

"Hope you don't mind if I spread my stuff out on your table," Daniel said, pointing to the maps. "The one upstairs in my room is a bit small, and I've got my computer set up there."

Annie walked over and said, "Of course not, we use this table mostly for breakfasts out here in warm weather anyway. Would you like some coffee or hot chocolate? It's a bit chilly outside."

He looked up at her and they locked eyes. Sometimes in a person's life, you meet someone and you know – somehow – that the two of you are 'simpatico', as his mother had said. Annie was one of those people and he'd known it the minute he laid eyes on her. But he was here on business and couldn't let his personal life get in the way – not now, at least. Maybe later... "Hot chocolate please, if you'll join me," he said, smiling.

"Happy to," she replied and went back inside to make their hot chocolate. Upon returning, she placed his mug near him and glanced at the maps. Leaning over his shoulder she added, "Why, those are property maps! Are you thinking of buying something here on the island?" That prospect made her happy for some strange reason.

He shook his head. "No, as I mentioned on the phone, I'm here on business." He looked up at her. "But hopefully I can make a little time when that part's over to just relax for a couple of days..." He noticed her big brown eyes, how expressive they were, and her gentle voice.

She lit up. "That's great! Then, I hope that you get all finished up sooner rather than later!" *I wonder why I said that*, she thought. "That is, I mean to say, we all need some time off and this is a perfect place to relax!" She sat down near him and scanned the maps. "If I can be of any help, I'm pretty familiar with the island..."

Lies in the Sand

He was warmed by her offer. "That's very kind of you, Annie. Actually, the reason I'm here is because my company sent me to appraise a piece of land that's going to be auctioned off soon – just north of your place, I believe…" he said, studying the map and pointing to the lots involved.

Annie's heart went cold. That auction really was going to happen, and this man was here to facilitate the business! All kinds of thoughts rushed through her mind: maybe she could influence him and get the price down (*Of course not, that's silly and wouldn't work*…) Maybe she could get him to help her get the right bid in (*again, not very ethical*…) Maybe she could just shoot him and bury his body in the sand and this auction would never happen (**shut up, Annie, what are you thinking**!). "Could I ask who owns the land now?" she managed to squeak out.

"I'm sorry, but I can't tell you that, this is a private auction." He looked around and made a quick decision. "But I can tell you this," he said quietly, "the attorneys told us that the owner just inherited this land and is only interested in one thing: getting the best price he can." He shook his head. "I don't understand why anyone who inherited something this…beautiful," he said, looking out at the ocean, "would be in a hurry to sell it. But then, that's not my business, I suppose…" He shrugged.

Annie tilted her head and raised one eyebrow. "What if you had inherited it, Daniel, what would you do with it?"

He thought for a moment. "Well, I'd probably use the land as collateral, build a nice beach house and come here as often as I could!" He grinned at her. "I'd live right next door to you then!"

She smiled sadly. "Then I'm sorry that it's not yours to buy, Daniel…"

He nodded. "Yep, me too. But me bidding on this property would not be ethical – or maybe even legal." He exhaled loudly. "Oh, well, a man can dream!"

Annie laughed and then helped him study the maps. But the resentment she felt for this whole sudden upheaval in her life had just found a person to land on. A very nice and good-looking person, but still…

Lies in the Sand

    The fire of anger in her belly came back to life. She'd worked too hard on her dream to have it ruined by some greedy landowner who cared nothing about the Outer Banks!

Lies in the Sand

Chapter 15

Soon the other guests arrived and Annie was busy for several hours getting everyone all settled in. A newlywed couple from Ohio rented one room; an older couple celebrating their thirtieth anniversary had taken the room with the best view for a long weekend; and the remaining room was taken by a single woman, a professional from Norfolk who'd been here several times and was coming back to the beach to de-stress. All in all, they seemed a compatible lot who would be easy enough to please, Annie decided. She set about planning menus and making all the necessary arrangements.

Terry would be coming in tomorrow to help with breakfast and clean the rooms, and she could tell her friend all the news about the property then. Daniel came down and asked for a recommendation for a good restaurant nearby; Annie named several and gave him the lowdown on the best dishes each place served. He nodded and walked toward the door, but then turned back. "Uh...would you like to join me for dinner, Annie?" he asked, grinning. "My treat!"

She hesitated. "Maybe another time, Daniel, thanks. I've got a lot to do tonight to get ready for tomorrow morning. But thanks for the offer." Despite trying hard to hate him, she really wanted to go spend time with this guy. But she had her 'Rule No. 1': she didn't get romantically involved with her visitors and there were no exceptions. Although, if she'd ever been tempted to break it, this was the time... "Enjoy your dinner!" she said and turned away quickly before she changed her mind.

He nodded and waved, then walked out the door.

The next morning Daniel was up early. He decided to go out and walk the auction property thoroughly, looking for anything that might be helpful to get this business taken care of. He was tying on his shoes when Annie spotted him out on the porch. She had to at least try to find out how things were going, so she walked out and took the rocker next to Daniel's.

"Sleep well?" she asked. "How is your room?"

Daniel's train of thought suddenly changed tracks. He smiled at her. "I slept great! Even though I don't have an ocean view, I could still hear the surf, and it lulled me to sleep. The room is great, the bed is comfortable, and I couldn't be happier."

"Going for a walk on the beach?" she asked.

"Yes, well, sort of. I watched the sunrise and now I need to walk the property and try to determine approximately where the property lines are, if possible. You see, I'm making up a colorful brochure to highlight the location, beauty and potential of the property. Whoever buys it will be sending out a survey team, but I'd like to get a general idea of the boundaries and the property's good points, as well as any problems a buyer might encounter. That way I can make up a report that gives any potential buyer a realistic picture, more than just the facts."

"That's very wise of you," she said, nodding. "So many people buy homes down here and have no idea about what living on the beach is like. They come here thinking that everything will be paradise, and then the reality hits them. We have floods from nor'easters and hurricanes, power outages from time to time, and well… it's a remote area with a laid-back lifestyle that most city folks just don't understand until they've been here a while."

"I might not mention all that in the brochure," he said, grinning at her. "What are the winters like?" he asked.

"Cold. *Windy*! Especially January through March, that's when we get the coldest weather, even snow occasionally. And did I mention the wind?" she asked smiling. "It comes in off the ocean, cold and damp, and wind speeds can get high. It blows in your ears, up your nose, and can chill you right to the bone. This past winter we even had a 'snowicane', what the weather people called a 'bomb cyclone'. It was bad!" She raised her shoulders and pretended to be cold.

Lies in the Sand

He raised his eyebrows. "Wow! I never thought..."

She nodded. "Most people don't. But those few months of cold weather don't last long. Then we have a beautiful spring, a spectacular summer and then a lovely fall; so, winter's not all that bad." She had to be honest with him.

Her enthusiasm was contagious. "You love it here, don't you?" he asked.

She grinned. "My parents inherited the land, built this house when I was young and we came here every chance we got. They retired here, but then Mom had a heart attack and died. Not long after, Dad got sick and seemed to just...fade away." She looked off into the distance. "I guess he didn't want to go on without her." She wiped away a tear that slid down her cheek. "Sorry... even after all this time, it still hurts to remember some parts of it..."

He took her hand. "I understand, really I do. Both my parents were killed in an accident a few years ago. They were looking forward to retirement and then – suddenly – it was all changed. My whole family is still trying to get over it, but I guess you never really do. Losing your parents makes you feel..." he struggled for words.

"Like an orphan?" she said.

He nodded. "Yes, like an orphan who's been abandoned. That's crazy I know – it not's like they left us on purpose – but still you have those feelings. My two younger sisters have really taken it hard. Mom and Dad didn't even get to meet any of their grandchildren..." He looked away, his eyes moist.

She squeezed his hand. "It's nice to talk to somebody who understands."

He put his other hand on top of hers. "Yes, it sure is." He gave her his best smile, directly from his heart.

Annie sat up and slowly removed her hand from between both of his. "Well, if you need me to walk with you, just say so. I can find the time after I get done with breakfast."

"You sure?" he asked.

"Absolutely. I can probably tell you more about this place than anyone else around here." She looked up. "Except for Finis – he's the expert. Been here his whole life – he's a native 'Banker' and his folks came over on whatever ship landed here first, I think!" she said, smiling and drying her eyes. "He's a character, though, I'm warning you ahead of time!" She gave him a mischievous grin.

Daniel smiled. "Can't wait to meet him! I'm a country boy myself and all those old coots around where I grew up over in the state's western mountains taught me early-on how to get along with his type."

"Where are you from?" she asked. "Asheville?"

He grinned. "Nowhere near a city; it was more or less a holler in the Smoky Mountains, to be honest with you. Kind of a village, but not really. One man had a store that sold necessities, but you had to go into Waynesville if you needed anything, or even Asheville if you needed a city. Lots of moonshiners and a few pot-growers around. To tell you the truth, my heritage is pure hillbilly!"

She laughed. "Well, you'll have to tell me more about the place, but right now I have to get breakfast ready. You hungry?" She stood up.

"Starved, actually. It must be the ocean air!"

"Well, Daniel Marcus, you won't be starved for long, I can promise you that. Just come back from your walk soon, and you'll see more breakfast than you can imagine!" She turned and walked toward the kitchen.

"I'm sure I'll love it – I love everything about this place!" he blurted out.

Annie smiled at him as she walked toward the kitchen. She really wanted to hate this guy and do everything that she could to stop his work, but he was growing on her by the minute. *Keeping Rule No. 1 was not going to be easy this time...*

Chapter 16

After a huge breakfast of fruit, ham, eggs, hash browns and pastries, Daniel needed to get up and move. So, he took off for the beach and told Annie he'd come back and get her in a little while. She waved him off and got to work in the kitchen with Terry.

"So…" Terry began. "Who's the hunk?" She gave Annie her most innocent look. "Is he married?"

Annie grinned. "Oh, shut up, Terry, you know that I never break Rule No.1, and besides, he's here on business!"

"Hmmm…. well, he's sweet and I've got no such silly rule…" She glanced sideways and watched her friend's reaction.

Annie frowned and said, "Well, uh, whatever…"

Terry snickered. "Just as I figured! You like him, don't you?"

Annie's head snapped around. "Terry! You know that I don't do that! He's a really nice guy, and to tell you the truth, I'm not even sure if he's married – we never discussed that, and I'm not about to ask!" She went back to her dishes.

Terry laughed and began to hum a tune. Annie wouldn't try to find out if he was single, but she could – and she would. *After all, what are friends for?*

Daniel walked into the kitchen later and asked Annie if she could get away and go for that walk with him. She told him it would be a minute, but she'd be happy to go. He nodded, stepped out, and she removed her apron and hung it on the wall.

Lies in the Sand

"Walk on the beach, huh?" Terry asked innocently.

Annie put her hands on her hips. "It's not like that, Terry! He needs to get familiar with the property lines and the lay of the land, and I told him that I'd help him, that's all!"

"If you say so," Terry answered, grinning. "But that sounds like aiding the enemy, I'm surprised you're doing it..."

Me, too! Annie thought, shaking her head and wondering how she'd gotten herself tied into this mess. Annie made a huffy sound and then went to find Daniel. Terry knew her better than anyone, and she could hit pretty close to home when she wanted to. Besides, Terry could never resist a situation to make her friend squirm a little.

As they walked down the dunes to the beach, Daniel stopped suddenly and said, "Oh, I forgot my compass – I'll be right back!" He turned and ran toward the porch. Annie stood looking out at the ocean as she waited for him to return. The sun was up, the waves were fairly gentle and the tide was out. This was a good time to walk around on the beach. She truly loved this place, and the thought of another house, or even worse some kind of 'touristy' place moving in next door, broke her heart.

As much as she wanted to hate Daniel and his company, it was not going to be easy. He was just doing his job, after all. If it hadn't been him, it would have been someone just like him – well, not just like him because he was a special kind of man. She'd only known him less than a day and already she could see that.

"Okay, I'm ready," Daniel said as he plowed through the sand toward Annie.

"You actually use a compass?" she asked, teasing him. "Do you have some pirate blood in you by any chance?"

He squinted one eye closed and said in a raspy voice, "Ye can nevva be sure, Lass, so don't be crossin' me, now, or I'll take my sword and cut off all that beautiful hair of yours!" He grinned at her and flipped a few strands of her hair. She laughed out loud. Daniel had a great sense of humor, and made her laugh easily.

He took out his compass and began walking north. Suddenly he stopped and tapped it. Then he shook it and tapped it again. "Hey, come look at this!" he said.

Annie walked up and looked down at his compass. The needle was moving erratically. "What's going on?"

He shook his head. "I don't know! What's to break on a compass? It always points north." He shook it again, but it stayed the same. "Oh, well, I don't suppose I really need it, that way is north, right?" He pointed toward a spot out in the ocean.

She took his arm and directed it to the right a little. "More like that, I think. At least that's what my last survey said. But they never mentioned anything about a compass not working here."

He scrunched up his face. "Well, surveyors use satellites and digital equipment these days, so they probably don't even bring old-fashioned compasses with them anymore. This one belonged to my grandfather and he gave it to me. It's pretty old, but I don't understand how it could 'break.' It's always pointed true north, and when you're lost in the mountains, that's a mighty handy thing to know!" He shrugged and put the compass in his shirt pocket. "Oh, well, just show me around if you will, that'll be fine for now."

"Of course, this way."

They walked to a place that Annie said was the edge of her property. Her grandparents had bought three lots back in the day, and she owned one of the best parcels around. The house sat smack-dab in the middle and she'd been tempted to sell off one of the other lots, but couldn't bring herself to do it. The surrounding dunes and sea oats were part of the charm of the place to her. And being right up next to one of those big fifteen-bedroom monstrosities was not what her visitors expected. They liked the extra privacy and were willing to pay a little more to have it.

She headed north, paced off the approximate size of four lots and turned around. "This is the farthest point that it could be, Daniel, if the new owner has four lots, like you said. But if it's fewer, then it would be proportionately smaller."

He nodded. "I'm sure that it's four lots, but I'm not sure of the size of them. Let's walk up on the dunes and see the lay of the land." They headed up that way and into the scrubby trees and light foliage. "What kind of trees are these?" he asked, rubbing his fingers over a leaf hanging nearby.

She shrugged. "Some kind of oak, I'd say, but I'm no arborist. Finis could tell you, he knows all about the local flora and fauna." She kicked at the sand. "One thing I do know about is these sand-spurs, or stickers as some people call them – they're everywhere and getting them off of you is a nasty business."

He looked down at his socks. "Hmmm…. looks like some of them have formed an attachment to me!"

She laughed. "Get used to it if you're tracking around the dunes, buddy, they are everywhere!"

He bent down to pluck one off his socks. "Ouch! That little sucker hurts!" He put his finger in his mouth.

Annie laughed. "I guess you don't have many of those in the Smoky Mountains, huh?"

"No, we've got 'beggarlice' and all kinds of other things that grab onto your clothes, but these little boogers are something different!" His thumb was still stinging, so he decided to wait until later to pick off the rest of them on his shoes and socks.

"Beggarlice? You catch lice in the woods?" Annie made a face.

Daniel laughed. "No, they're not lice, or insects of any kind. They're like these things, a seed of a plant that comes with little stickers to attach it to whatever comes by; it's how the seeds are spread. With beggarlice, they're like Velcro, you have to peel 'em off one at a time. But they don't have teeth, like these do!"

Lies in the Sand

They looked at each other and laughed. It was a beautiful spring day; they walked around for a half hour or so and then sat down on a dune overlooking the water and talked for a long time, each sharing stories of where they grew up. Time passed quickly this way.

Annie stood up and dusted off her pants. "Well, I've got a business to run and as much as I love being out here, I'd better get inside," she said. "But this has been fun, Daniel, I have to say."

"I'll walk you back. I need to pick up some more equipment and my tablet to take photos and make notes."

When they came through the back door, Terry was standing there with towels in her arms. "Mr. Marcus, you're in Room Four, right?"

He nodded as he untied his sandy shoes. "Yep, that's me."

"Will your wife be joining you this weekend? If so, I can leave extra towels in your bath." She gave him an innocent look.

"No, no, I'm not married, it's just me," he said, removing his shoes.

Terry looked at Annie and grinned, and then took off upstairs. Annie shook her head. "Sorry, she's the nosey type…"

He looked confused. "She's just doing her job, right? No problem." He shrugged.

Daniel got a call from Ron, his boss in Raleigh. The seller was anxious to have the auction and was pressuring the company to get it done ASAP. The office manager was clearly aggravated with the man's attitude and pushiness and she was getting tired of fielding his calls. Daniel exhaled slowly; he didn't even know this Felix Benefield person and already didn't like him. Well, liking him wasn't his job, this was, so he'd just get on with it.

That afternoon he visited the Dare County Register of Deeds office in Manteo. The ladies there were helpful, but there seemed to be something a little 'off' about the history of the deed, so he asked them to examine the case personally. They agreed, but told him that there were a few other cases ahead of his and it would take time. He knew that Felix Benefield was not going to like that! Daniel asked why the last owner's title search had not turned up this little glitch.

The Dare County people explained to him that when the National Park Service bought up the land back in the 1950's, deeds and titles for Hatteras Island had been a hit-and-miss sort of thing. The folks on this island had done things their own way for a long, long time and often their way didn't fit in with the government's way of doing things. So, a lot of the dealing had been done 'back room' style to accommodate the locals. But by the time it was finished, all the property for the National Seashore had been obtained one way or another.

Well, this wasn't Daniel's first rodeo by any means, so he'd just do his best to try to play nice with the folks in the office and get it worked out as soon as possible. In the meantime, his paperwork would be on hold until that part was settled. He decided to go back, take more photos and begin work on the brochure.

That evening all the guests sat around chatting and sharing wine, and the remainder of the day passed without any more private conversation between Annie and Daniel. The current group of visitors were outgoing and friendly, and the older couple really enjoyed sharing funny marriage stories with the newlyweds. They gathered around the fire until late at night, and then everyone went upstairs.

Chapter 17

The following morning Daniel was up early again, as was his habit. He went walking the property before breakfast again and wound up over on the highway boundary. As before, he took out his compass and the needle seemed to do the same thing as before – just jump around, unable to come to a rest in any direction. As he paced up and down the pavement, holding the compass different ways and in many directions, he heard a voice.

"Your compass ain't workin' now, is it?" someone yelled.

He looked up. Standing across the road was an old man with his arms crossed. Daniel smiled and waved. "I'm sorry, what did you say?" he asked.

The old fellow looked aggravated. "Ain't no sense in tryin' to make it work neither, you gotta get at least a half-mile away from here in either direction before it'll start to settle down!" the old man said, making a face.

"Uh… hello, my name is – " Daniel began.

"Don't care!" the man hollered. "Don't want to know."

Daniel cocked his head to the side and stared. This must be the old guy that Annie had told him about – the local who knew so much about the area. She'd said that he might not make a great first impression and she'd been right! Undeterred, Daniel walked across the road and made his way slowly toward the man.

"So, what makes it act this way?" Daniel asked, holding out his compass. He walked right up to the fellow and held out the compass. The old man stared at him sternly for a few long moments, then reluctantly reached out and took the antique piece. "Have you had the same thing happen to you?" Daniel pressed.

The man looked up and glared at him. "Hold your horses, boy, I ain't even had time to look at your compass here!"

Lies in the Sand

"Yessir." Daniel hung his head.

After handling the compass, turning it this way and that admiringly, the man said, "This here's a Dollard compass, a mighty old one at that! Where'd you get this?"

"My grandfather gave it to me, Sir. I think that he said it had been passed down to him, but I'm not certain about that – I was just a boy when he died. It's got a nice wooden box to keep it in, but I always use it when I go out scouting around because Paw-Paw said that good tools need to be used, not stored away so nobody sees 'em."

"He sounds like a wise man, your grandfather," the old man said, looking up at Daniel's face and scrutinizing him carefully.

"Yessir, he was that. And so was my father, God rest his soul." Daniel was pulling out all his homespun charm to make a little headway with this old man. But still, the wrinkled, gray-haired fellow just stood there, sizing Daniel up.

Daniel stuck out his hand, "Name's Daniel Marcus, Sir, from Raleigh, originally from the western mountains of North Carolina."

"Well, I'll try not to hold that against you." The old fella stared at Daniel's extended hand until he put it back down. "Whatcha' doin' here, boy?"

Daniel stood up straight. This guy was not an easy nut to crack... "My company sent me out to appraise that piece of land across the road there," he said, turning and pointing. "It's going to be auctioned off soon, and they needed to get eyes on it so we could make up a nice flyer for the auction."

The old man handed Daniel's compass back to him and crossed his arms again. "Never happen!"

"Excuse me, Sir, what did you just say?" Daniel asked, looking confused.

"I said," he began, looking at Daniel with pity, "that it ain't never gonna happen! There'll be no auction! You deaf or just plain stupid?"

Not knowing exactly how to respond to that, Daniel stood there with his mouth hanging open.

"Yep. Stupid, just like I figured," the old man said, and then he turned and walked away.

Trying to think of some way to salvage this quickly deteriorating situation, Daniel called out, "Sir, can I ask you some more questions, please?"

"Nope!" the man said and kept walking.

"I didn't catch your name!" Daniel tried one last time.

"That's 'cause I didn't throw it," he said, flapping his hand over his shoulder without turning around and continued walking away.

Daniel watched the man as he slowly made his way south alongside the road. He'd met some crusty old-timers before, but this one took the cake! He laughed, shook his head, and walked back across the street to take some more photos.

After breakfast, he took Annie aside. "I believe I met your friend, the old guy who knows so much," he said, grinning.

"Finis?" she said, her eyebrows up high. "Finis actually talked to you?"

"Well, I talked to him and he spared me a few words. Not the best conversationalist I've ever met, and a touch on the rude side…" he said, shaking his head slowly.

Annie laughed out loud, putting her hand over her mouth. "Yes, that was probably him! He must like you," she said, smiling.

"*Like me*?" Daniel asked, surprised. "I wouldn't want to see how he treated people that he didn't like!"

"No, you wouldn't," she said, grinning. "He goes out of his way to avoid tourists. Come over here and sit down and let me tell you about Finis." She motioned him toward one of the sofas.

Lies in the Sand

"What kind of name is...how did you pronounce that exactly?" Daniel asked, grabbing a sofa pillow and holding it in front of him for defense from the old man, who was nowhere near.

"You say 'Fi'-ness'. He'll tell you that story someday maybe, and when he does, you can be sure that he does like you at that point!"

Daniel shook his head a few times.

Annie said, "Okay, look: Finis is like a lot of other old guys; he's rough on the outside and soft on the inside."

"Well, the inside certainly doesn't show..." Daniel put in.

She raised her hand. "Not at first, and definitely not to strangers. But I've known him since I was a little girl. He didn't like having somebody build a house across the road from his property and he let my father know that right off the bat. But Dad wore him down eventually, and Mom learned what his favorite desserts were and made them whenever we'd come. She always sent me over there with two slices of whatever it was – one for him and one for his wife."

Annie smiled. "So, they both got to liking me pretty fast. When I moved back here, he was happy to see me fixing up the old place and told me not to let any 'trashy-like people' stay here with me." She grinned, remembering his reaction. "But if he spoke to you at all the first time and didn't walk off, that's a good sign," she said nodding. "He must like the look of you."

"Coulda fooled me, that's for sure! Maybe it was Paw-Paw's compass that he liked – he actually held it and examined it reverently, and *almost* shook my hand. He knew that it was an antique Dollard," he said, holding it out for Annie to see.

She took the small antique device and looked at it closely. "This is old! Yeah, that's the kind of thing that gets his attention, alright. Especially anything maritime like this." She handed it back. "I'll take you over there and introduce you to him. He's really not that bad..."

Lies in the Sand

He held up his hand. "Thanks, I believe I'll pass on that one. But then, wait a minute, he did say something that I didn't understand. He said 'ain't never gonna happen' when I told him there would be an auction. I'd like to know what he meant by that and why he said it."

Annie caught her bottom lip with her teeth as she contemplated that. *How adorable*, Daniel thought. "Well, I sure have no idea," she said. "But with Finis, he doesn't say stuff like that without a reason. Seems like I remember Dad saying something about a curse…or some local legend like that. It's been so long, I can't remember. Like I said, Finis is the one who knows this place and its history."

"Yes!" He held up his pointer finger. "And he also knew that the compass wouldn't work. He told me I'd have to go at least half a mile down the road in either direction for it to work right!" He scratched his head. "I wonder what's going on with that?"

Annie shrugged. "You'll find that there's all kinds of odd things out on the Outer Banks. All kinds of legends, mysteries, folklore and just plain made-up rubbish that people like to tell. Especially the old-timers. It must have been their entertainment back in the day." She looked around. "I've gotta get busy, paperwork to catch up on," she said, rising. "But we can go over to his place in the afternoon for a bit, if you like?"

Daniel had to give a little thought to that not-so-pleasant offer. But spending time with Annie was fun, and she'd be there to run interference for him with the old guy, so why not? "Just knock on my door when you have the time. I've got some reports to write up myself." He stood up and walked toward the stairs. He stopped, turned and said, "Thanks, Annie! It's a date!" He gave her his best smile before heading upstairs.

It's a date? she thought. *Wait a minute, that's not what I meant…*

About that time, Terry stuck her head out from the kitchen doorway. "I couldn't help but overhear… so, you've got a date?" she asked, grinning.

Annie picked up the sofa pillow that Daniel had put down and threw it at her smart-aleck friend. Terry ducked back inside, just in time, and Annie heard her giggling like a little girl in the kitchen.

Lies in the Sand

Chapter 18

Around three o'clock, Annie stacked up her papers, shut down her computer and stood up, stretching her back and neck. She didn't really mind paperwork, but she'd come to learn that being self-employed entailed a lot more of it than she'd imagined. The government forms seemed to be never-ending. But then, she was her own boss and even though her hours were long, she's the one who set them.

She knocked on Daniel's door and heard him push the chair back and walk over. He opened the door wide and she noticed that his room was neat, not perfectly clean, but neat, especially for a single man. *Another plus in his favor!*

"Ready to go?" he asked, grabbing his jacket.

She nodded. "I've got a little time now. Finis' place isn't far, so let's walk."

"Great!"

They crossed the two-lane road and walked south for a few hundred yards. Annie turned down a sandy driveway and they walked back toward the Pamlico Sound. "We get the loveliest sunsets over the water out here," she said wistfully. "Some days the colors are breathtaking, you just wouldn't believe it unless you saw it." She turned to him. "Maybe we'll get some good ones while you're here. Keep an eye out about half an hour before dark. Your bedroom window is a great place to catch the view."

They passed another sandy drive that went off to the left. Daniel looked back in and thought he saw an old cottage back there. "Is that his place?" he asked, pointing in that direction.

"No, that place belonged to a relative of his, Mr. Midgett, who sold it last year to a young woman from up north somewhere. She married the local vet and they live in his house now, but they keep this place as a getaway," she said, smiling. "Nice people, both of them, you'd like them."

"Oh. How much farther to Finis' place?" he asked.

"Just a little way, down around that next bend."

The rutted road had scrubby-looking grass growing in the middle of the sandy tracks. Evidently it wasn't used a lot, and Daniel commented on that.

Annie laughed and said, "Oh, he's got a truck and he uses it, but he walks a lot. That's one of the reasons he's in as good a shape as he still is."

Daniel nodded and exhaled heavily. Meeting this man again was not high on his list of Things to Do on the Outer Banks'. They walked up to an old cottage, well-maintained, with a large porch. Crab pots and a weathered boat took up half the yard, and an old barn and a rusty pickup truck were on the other side.

Annie walked right up onto the porch and knocked on the front door. "Finis! You home?" she yelled out.

They heard what sounded like a groan and a grunt combined, and then someone shuffling toward the door. Finis opened it, saw Annie and smiled. Then he saw Daniel and his look changed immediately. "What'd you bring him here for?"

Annie gently pushed Finis aside and walked in, motioning for Daniel to follow. He hesitated, given the look he was getting from the old guy. After a long moment, Finis turned around and headed for his recliner, not saying yea or nay. Annie signaled him to come in, so Daniel closed the door behind him and stood against it, the knob in his hand behind his back, ready to make a quick getaway if the need arose.

"I brought him here to introduce him to you. Finis Turnbull, this is my friend Daniel Marcus from Raleigh. Daniel, my good friend Finis," she said, waving her hand back and forth.

Lies in the Sand

Finis grunted. Annie walked over, plopped down on the couch and turned to Finis, shaking her finger, her eyes squinted. "Now you be nice to him, Finis. He's a good guy, really he is."

Finis cleared his throat so loudly that Daniel thought he might have some kind of disorder. Then he turned toward Daniel and gave him a slight nod. *That must mean we're making progress*, Daniel thought. Daniel nodded back and smiled. Finis didn't smile.

"Well," Finis said, "what does he want, Annie? Is he some stranger trying to take advantage of you and your good nature?" Referring to the stranger in the third person, he gave her the protective-father look.

She laughed. "Of course not, Finis! He's just here to do his job, to appraise that property next to mine. Evidently, it's for sale now..." She looked down.

"Never happen!" Finis grunted, shaking his head vigorously.

"That's what you said this morning!" Daniel said. "Why do you say that, Mr. Turnbull? What is it that makes you think it can't be sold?"

Finis looked him over good. He turned to Annie. "Can that fella be trusted?"

She nodded. "I think so. He's a decent man, and you know that I'm a good judge of character."

"Well, if you say so..." Finis got comfortable in his chair and pointed at Daniel. "Now sit down, don't interrupt me with silly questions and I'll tell you the whole story, alright, boy?"

"Yessir, I promise," Daniel answered, moving over to sit beside Annie.

"My family's been in these parts since the white people first showed up, back in the 1700's. I got heroes, lifesavers, pirates and rapscallions of all kind in my bloodline. Mamma's people were from up here, and Daddy's folks were from the south end of Hat'tras Island. So, if there's somethin' to be known about this place, my family knew it!" He nodded his head slowly.

"My daddy and granddaddy told me, when I was but a boy, that-there piece of land was cursed," he said, pointing in the general direction of the property. "Said the curse went all the way to the days of Blackbeard, and – "

"Blackbeard the pirate?" Daniel blurted out.

Finis just looked at him. "You gonna let me tell this story or not?"

"Oh, sorry, I didn't mean to interrupt," Daniel said, looking guilty.

"Yes, you did!" Finis said. "But anyhow, nobody knows exactly what the curse is, but it's tied up with that piece of land," he said, nodding his head in that general direction. "It's said to go back to Blackbeard and some treasure he hid there, way back when. My father told me that when he was young he tried to go digging to find the treasure back in 1919, but then his mother got real sick that same day and died a few days later, so he believed the curse was real and never went near the place again."

Daniel opened his mouth to ask another question, but then shut it real fast.

"So..." Finis went on, "Daddy told me never to mess with it or go onto it, and I never have. He said all kinds of bad things happen to people who try to dig up Blackbeard's treasure! Now, I'm an old man, but I'm not stupid; if anybody goes messin' with that land, something bad's gonna happen to 'em. I'm certain of it. So, I tell you, nobody will buy or sell that cursed land. It's been sittin' there since the days of the Indians and it'll sit there from now on, just like it is. Everything will be alright if nobody messes with it!"

He leaned forward. "But if they do, something awful's gonna happen." He pointed to Annie. "And Annie's right next door to that place! I don't want nuthin to happen to Annie – she's a sweet girl and never hurt a soul. You understand me, boy?"

Daniel nodded briskly. Annie made a face and said, "Finis, you know that I don't believe in superstitious garbage like that! It's probably just some coincidences that caused the rumor about the curse! For instance, a lot of people on this island – all over the world, even - died of the Spanish Flu back in 1818-1819, not just your grandmother!"

Lies in the Sand

Finis sat back in his chair and crossed his arms. A strand of white hair fell onto his forehead and he stuck out his bottom lip and blew it away. "You can believe what you want. But, mark my words, that property will set right where it is from now on and nobody will molest it, because of the curse that hangs over it!"

Daniel cleared his throat and said, "Can I say something now please?"

Finis nodded and shrugged.

"I respect you and your opinion a great deal, Finis. And there *is* something odd about how that place affects a compass, for sure. There was an old letter that came with the deed that mentioned some kind of curse, but it didn't say much other than the fact that the place was cursed and whoever owned it should keep far away from it."

"Told you!" Finis muttered, pointing at Daniel.

Daniel nodded. "The letter didn't mention a treasure, though... could it be possible that Blackbeard was really around these parts back in those days to bury something there?" He asked. Annie looked at Daniel sideways. She couldn't believe that anybody would actually buy that hogwash about a curse!

Finis nodded. "Boy, Blackbeard was all over this island! He had a hideout down on Ocracoke and to this day they still have a 'Pirate Day' there every year dedicated to him! He was up and down the Outer Banks; had some kind of sweet deal with the governor of North Carolina, if I remember right. People here thought of him as some kind of superman." He shook his head. "He was vicious and bloodthirsty and King Charles' navy did everybody a favor when they cut off his head!" He punctuated that with a sharp head nod.

"Well," Daniel went on, "I'm a bit of a North Carolina history buff myself, but most of my studies have been focused on the settlement of the mountains, where I'm from. But I'd love to look into this and find out more about it. Do you have any recommendations for something to read or someone around here to talk to, Mr. Turnbull?"

Finis looked him up and down. "You serious? You not just playin' with me here, are you, boy?"

"No, sir! I'm curious now and since I'm down here for a week, I'd like to learn as much as I can about the history of the area."

Finis grunted and looked Daniel over once more. They all sat there quietly while the old man made up his mind. Finally, he said, "Alright, I'll take you around. There's one or two old-timers in these parts who know some things – not nearly as much as I do, you understand – but they dearly love to talk to anybody who'll sit still long enough to listen. You want to go for a ride?"

Daniel brightened. "Sure, can I go get my car and drive you around?"

Finis guffawed. "If we come driving up in that fancy car of yours, nobody'll talk to either one of us. It's got the look of guv'ment about it, and folks round here don't talk to guv'ment people if they can help it. No, we'll take my truck." He stood up slowly. "You goin' with us, Annie?" he asked, turning to her.

She stammered, still not believing that Daniel would want to get involved in this. "I...I... no, I've got to get back and go to work. You two have a nice time." She gave Daniel a 'what's-going-on-here' look and he grinned mischievously.

Finis grabbed a jacket and his keys and headed for the door. "Shut the door when you leave, Annie," he said as he walked out, Daniel following close behind.

"Uh huh," she murmured. She shook her head. Life was strange sometimes.

Chapter 19

The old truck started up much faster than Daniel had thought it would. As they rode south down the two-lane highway, Finis turned to Daniel and said, "If I find out you're playin' with me, or with that girl's feelings – either one – I want you to know that I got ways to hurt a man that you never even heard of. You understand me?" He glared.

"Yessir, I mean no sir, I'm not doing any of that, I swear!" Daniel said, putting out the palm of his right hand.

Finis grunted. "I'm old, but I'm not dead, boy! I seen the way you two look at each other!"

"There's nothing going on between us, I promise! Annie's a nice person but it's business – that's all!" Daniel said. Finis grunted. "Uh… where we headed?" Daniel asked, politely trying to shift the direction of this uncomfortable conversation.

"You'll know when we get there," Finis replied, driving the rickety old truck at no more than thirty miles per hour. Daniel noticed the play in the steering wheel and how Finis was wandering around on the road. He swallowed and tried to think positive. The man had lived this long, so luck must be with him and this old bucket that he drove around.

Nothing else was said until they pulled up at a bar called *The Rusty Anchor* and rolled to a stop on the gravel right in front of the door. Finis got out without saying a word, and Daniel followed him. They walked through the front door and he looked around. *What a dive! This place must be at least fifty years old!* Daniel thought. Well, he had signed up for this roller coaster ride, so he'd hang on til the end…

Lies in the Sand

"Pete!" Finis yelled. "You in here?"

Daniel heard shuffling coming from the back room. "Finis? Is that you, you old buzzard?" A man stuck his head into the room. "Sure enough, it is! What earth-shaking thing's happened to get you out of that house of yours? Somebody die? You kill somebody again?" He grinned broadly.

"Oh, shut up, Pete, I need to talk to you for a few minutes! Can you set for a spell?"

Pete nodded and walked behind the bar. "Ya'll want a beer?" he asked.

Daniel looked toward Finis for a response. Without hesitation, Finis said, "Yeah, a Miller Lite – and he'll have the same thing," he said, nodding toward Daniel. "He's buyin'." They both plopped down onto the old wooden, squeaky stools.

"You got it, Finis," Pete said as he drew the beer and set it in front of them both. Daniel looked at the golden liquid. He was more of a craft beer man himself, but he wasn't about to cross Finis on anything. He took a drink. *Not bad... maybe he really was a beer snob like his friends had said...*

"Thank you," he said politely to both men.

Pete took a seat on his old wooden stool behind the bar, slinging his ever-present bar rag over his left shoulder. Daniel could see that he was almost as old as Finis, but he seemed a lot more sociable. "Well, what's on your mind, fellas?" Pete asked, grinning.

Finis took a long drink of beer, wiped his mouth with the back of his hand and said, "This boy wants to know about Blackbeard." He nodded his head in Daniel's general direction.

Pete looked the young man over. Early thirties probably, dressed like a city slicker here on vacation. What in the world was Finis doing hanging out with this guy? He hated tourists and avoided them like the plague. Oh, well, maybe he was a relative or something. "There's a lot to tell; whatcha want to know? Oh, by the way, I'm Pete, this is my bar," he said, extending his hand.

Lies in the Sand

Finally, a friendly person! He shook his hand. "I'm Daniel Marcus from Raleigh. My company sent me here. I'm here to appraise a parcel of land on the south end of the National Seashore that's going up for auction soon." He pointed in that general direction.

Pete looked at Finis. *"That piece?* The one next to Annie's place?" he asked in a low voice.

Finis nodded and took another drink of his beer, saying nothing.

Pete turned back to Daniel and cleared his throat. "So, how can I help you, Daniel?"

Daniel looked from one old man to another. "Finis – uh, Mr. Turnbull, I mean, he told me that the place had a curse on it from back in the days when Blackbeard the Pirate buried his treasure there. I've seen a copy of the deed, and it comes together with an old handwritten letter from a previous owner. The letter doesn't mention a treasure, but it does warn the owner not to go near the property because of a curse of some kind, no specifics. So, I'd like some more information – anything you can tell me, really, about any of that. If you have a little time, that is…"

Pete looked off in the distance and then looked to Finis questioningly. Finis nodded and shrugged. Pete said, "Well, I got time, but at my age, I'm not sure how much…" He snickered; Daniel smiled. "Now, normally this kind of history stays around the island, especially this particular piece… you not plannin' to write a book or something, are you?"

Daniel held up his hands. "Oh, no, I'm no writer! It's just that I'd like to help Annie to get her hands on that property," he said, turning to Finis. "But please don't tell her that, now, 'cause I'm not supposed to have a dog in this fight. My boss would rake me over the coals if he found out!"

Finis made some kind of undistinguishable noise, took another long drink and nodded.

Turning back to Pete, Daniel continued. "Annie is a great person, and she's worked so hard on her business. She's afraid that they'll put up a junky tourist store there or something and she wants to buy the land. But if there's a *real* curse attached to it, I'd be the first one to wave her off. I can help her – or not, if you know what I mean..."

Pete nodded and smiled. He thought of Maggie, his girlfriend of over forty years, who lived down on Ocracoke Island. He saw the same look in Daniel's eyes when he talked about Annie that he'd had in his own eyes when he first met Maggie. He nodded. "I understand. Totally." He smiled. "Do you believe in curses and such things, Daniel?"

Daniel raised both shoulders and made a face. "Let's put it like this: I was raised in the mountains of western North Carolina in a holler where my family has lived for generations. Most everybody there was superstitious. Since I was a boy, I've been hearing things like 'throw salt over your shoulder if you spill some,' and 'don't walk under a ladder', 'seven years bad luck if you break a mirror,' and stuff like that. But to be truthful, I'm not sure I believe any of it. Let's just say that I ... respect... those kinds of things."

'Well, you're honest, I'll give you that," Pete said. He looked over at Finis, who tilted his head slightly, shrugged his shoulders and gave him a 'so-what?' look. Pete could tell that Finis was testing this boy for some reason. But then, nobody ever knew why Finis did the things he did...

Pete wiped the bar with his rag as he gathered his thoughts. "I've been here for over forty years, runnin' this bar. So, if there's a rumor to be had, I've probably heard it. I've even spread a few myself." He grinned and wiggled his eyebrows. "But most folks never heard this one, just a few of us know about it. I believe that's so because those of us who've heard about it, well, we just want to stay as far away from it as we can get. Blackbeard lost his head, you know? I mean, literally!"

Daniel nodded. Finis grunted agreement, finished his beer and held out his mug. Pete obediently refilled it and then sat back down. "Okay, now this is the way I heard it from an old-timer who's long since dead. He said that his family was related to the people who'd owned the land and that's how they knew about it. The story goes that right after Blackbeard buried his treasure there, he went to Ocracoke and got himself killed. Then, through the years, a few more people tried to find the treasure. But they said that anybody who got close to it wound up hurt or killed as well."

Pete looked out the large window. "It's the lure of the treasure that keeps the story alive I think, but nobody knows anything for sure. Over the years, the story's taken some twists and turns, but the bottom line is that anybody who knows anything about it never goes there – just in case, you understand. But this is the first I've heard about a letter." He tilted his head.

"So, who did it belong to, do you know?" Daniel asked.

Pete shook his head. "Word is, somebody bought it back along the line so that they could have the treasure, but then the attempts to find it have all ended up so badly that they passed the deed and the warning about the curse down the family line. I have no idea who owns it these days." He shook his head. "And you have to remember that all this information is colored by generations of a family telling and re-telling it."

Daniel said, "Well, some guy just found out that he's inherited it and he wants to auction it off as fast as possible to get the cash. So, somebody's gonna be the new owner." He looked down at his beer. "Annie doesn't believe in any of that stuff about a curse – hogwash, she called it – but if there's any truth to it…"

Pete nodded. "Hmmm…. I understand. Did you hear the part about how the place messes with a compass?"

Daniel nodded. "Yeah, in fact I noticed it myself the second time I went out there to look around. My old compass needle bounced around like it was drunk!"

Finis belched loudly, then said, "Yep. Happens every time."

Daniel asked Pete, "Why do you think that happens? I mean, there's got to be a reason…"

Pete shrugged. "Above my pay grade, young man. But I have seen the compass needle jumpin' around for myself, so I know it's real, and it's a pretty weird thing to witness. I've only been near there on the beach that one time, and I'll never go again! I get the heebie-jeebies just talkin' about it!"

Finis turned to Daniel and stared at him. "Well?"

Daniel wasn't sure exactly what the question meant, but he tried to tread water. "Mr. Turnbull, I appreciate you taking the time to bring me here, I really do. And it's good to meet you, Pete, thanks for your time. I believe that I'll go back and see what I can dig up from the property office in Manteo, if anybody there knows anything."

Finis shook his head. "You won't find nuthin' there, I guarantee you. Ain't many people know about the curse." Noticing the look on Daniel's face he added, "Aw, go ahead and do what you have to, you will anyway. But like I said, don't be tellin' anybody about the buried treasure. Last thing we need around here is a bunch of treasure hunters tearing up the place!" He finished his second beer and plopped the mug on the table. "How's Maggie doin' Pete? Still runnin' that little shop down on Ocracoke?"

While Pete and Finis shared small talk, Daniel thought about what he'd heard. It was an odd story, to be sure, but could he find out what was behind it? So much of that kind of lore was lost in history and there was simply no way to dig out the roots of it, but he had to try...

Finis announced that it was time to go and got up, so Daniel quickly threw down a twenty-dollar bill and obediently followed. The old fella drove back to his house, weaving quite a bit more on the return trip. But he had a grin on his wrinkled face, and if it took a couple of Miller Lites to put it there, Daniel would remember that and make a run to the store to pick up a twelve-pack!

Chapter 20

When Daniel got back, Annie cornered him and nodded for him to follow her out to the porch. He obediently sat down in the wooden rocker and waited for whatever was to come.

She fidgeted for a while and then said, "Daniel, I appreciate that you want to… that is, that you're trying to… well, I'm not sure *what* it is that you're doing, to tell the truth!" She looked over at him. "What exactly *are* you doing, getting all involved in this silly business of a curse? You know that kind of nonsense is only for ignorant, uneducated minds!"

Daniel thought for a moment; this would have to be carefully put. "Well, I don't actually believe in curses and all that, but behind stories like this one there's usually some basis in fact that started the whole thing. Not saying that it's a curse – no, I don't believe that, but there's *something* that happened back in the past that caused people to believe there was a curse."

Annie make a snorting sound.

"Look, Annie, there's no conspiracy here, just me trying to dig out some facts. And Finis, well, he's not ignorant, he's just trying to protect you on all levels – from the curse, from me, from whatever he can! He obviously cares about you a great deal."

She sat up and turned toward him. "I don't *need* anybody to protect me! I'm a grown woman, I own my own business, and I can take care of myself, thank you very much!"

He spoke softly and tried to calm her down. "Yes, that's all true. And I don't believe that you need protection. But you must know that when men care about women, it's a natural instinct to want to protect them. And Finis obviously cares about you – that's why he doesn't want you to get involved with this property."

She sat back, crossing her arms. "He's a good old soul underneath all that gruff and bluster, that's true…"

"Yes, and he doesn't want anything bad to happen to you – it's obvious that he thinks of you as a daughter, a very dear friend. So, I wanted him to like me, too, and if you haven't noticed, that's a monumental undertaking, getting Finis' approval!" He grinned at her. "So, I tried to humor him. Besides, I *am* curious about the compass's reaction. That's peculiar and there must be some kind of explanation for it. I've got an old college buddy who teaches geology over at UNC, and I'm going to call him and ask about it. You don't mind if I do that, do you?"

She softened a bit. "Of course not, Daniel, I'd like to know about that part myself, because there's a perfectly rational explanation, I'm sure. But this is the twenty-first century and all this business about pirates and curses, it's just too 'out-there' for me! She waved her hand around in the air.

He grinned. "Look, I've only been here for a few days. I'm going to call my boss and ask for some vacation time so I can stay a little longer. I can email him all the data I get, together with the finished file for the brochure. Would it be okay with you if I stayed longer? Here?"

She smiled. "Of course. The couples are both leaving tomorrow, and the single woman's staying until Tuesday, but she keeps to herself so I'm sure she won't care either way. I'll be glad to have you here, Daniel."

He silently said *"Yes!"* to himself. "Alright, then, let me talk to my buddy Chad about the geological aspect and see what he has to say about it. We'll start from there, and see where it goes, okay?"

"Okay, but don't mention a treasure, please. That's the last thing we need, treasure hunters poking around." She reached over and patted his hand. "And thanks for your concern for me. This whole thing came out of the blue and has me confused and a little upset. I appreciate your calming influence."

He reached over and covered her hand with his. "It'll all work out, you'll see. I promise." He gave her his most reassuring smile and she could feel her heart beginning to melt. *There goes Rule No. 1,* she said to herself. *Terry's gonna have a field day with this!*

That night Daniel called his friend Chad, who was so excited about the compass mystery that he wanted to drive over the next day and see it for himself. Annie agreed that he could have a room, and the following morning Chad arrived before lunch.

Lies in the Sand

Chapter 21

Annie liked Chad right away. He was obviously a bit of a nerd, but he was a charming one, and so excited about geology that his enthusiasm was infectious. Besides, he would probably have a logical explanation for the compass thing, and then they could all go back to the original problem of the auction.

That afternoon Chad and Daniel went out together to explore the property. It was just four lots, but they were quite large ones; there were several sand dunes and scrubby trees offering a bit of shade. Daniel showed him the compass' reaction, then waited while his friend worked. Chad did a few simple soil tests and then got out some kind of a complicated-looking metal detector.

After a while, Chad came to sit beside Daniel on the dune, to watch the surf come in. "It's beautiful here – I wish I could afford this property!" he said to Daniel. "But this kind of piece is going to go for big money, and that's way out of my reach!" He leaned back on his elbows. "I believe I'll stay a few extra days if Annie has room. She's a great gal. And pretty, too."

Daniel turned to look at him. Chad was a nerd, but a good-looking one and he was single. "Yes, she is. In fact, *I think* she's quite special."

Chad pushed his glasses up on his nose and grinned. "I thought you might. No worries there, Bro, I'm just here for the exciting rocks!"

Daniel rolled his eyes. If his feelings for her were that obvious, he was in over his head. Oh, well, some things in life you just can't see coming... "So, what's the verdict on the exciting-rocks?"

Chad picked up a twig of sea oats and put it in his mouth. He laid back and rested his head on his hands, watching the clouds. "I hate to admit this, Daniel, but I don't know..."

"What? You, a well-known geologist and teacher, have no idea?" Daniel pretended to be flabbergasted.

Chad laughed. "Yeah, well, I got some ideas, but I want to talk to some of my professional contacts and run it by them. What I'm thinking is pretty far-out, and if it's true, then this is a big deal we got here."

"Give me a hint?" Daniel asked, perturbed. After all, he'd been the one to invite Chad out here.

"Nope. Mainly because I don't want to look like an idiot if it's not what I think it is." He looked at Daniel. "I'm a geology professor, you know, I'm supposed to have all the answers. If my students or peers ever found out that I'd made wild geological claims like some ignorant hick – and then proved to be wrong about it – well, I'd never hear the end of it! So, let's just say it's a mystery at this point." He closed his eyes and enjoyed the sun.

Daniel was a bit irritated by Chad's unwillingness to give up information. He got up, wiped the sand off his pants, and if a little of it landed on Chad's face, well, he didn't mind that. "I'm headed back. See you later. We'll go for dinner – I found a great seafood place." He walked away.

Chapter 22

Annie agreed to go to dinner with Chad and Daniel. *If there were three of them, it wouldn't seem like a date, would it?* After their food was served, Chad laid into his meal like he hadn't eaten in days. Annie looked at Daniel, her eyebrows raised.

"He always eats like that," Daniel said. "Don't know how he stays so thin, and some day it's gonna catch up with him." He grinned.

"Yadnn myet," Chad said, talking with his mouth full. Annie and Daniel looked at him in confusion. He swallowed and said, "I said, 'It hasn't yet.' I weigh the same thing as I did in college." He went back to his fries.

"I hate you," Annie said, with a smile on her face.

They discussed the auction, Chad's work, and the personal history of the two men. Chad had been on the phone earlier with a few fellow geologists from Washington, D.C., ones who were well-known in their field. Their thinking was in line with this, but there was only one way to verify their theory and it wasn't going to be easy. As hard as she tried to pry information out of him, Chad avoided answering any questions about the property. All he'd say was that they'd find out something soon.

"Daniel, is he always this… cagey?" she asked. "Seems like he's on a covert mission of some kind, doesn't it?" she teased.

"Absolutely," Daniel said. "Hey, Chad did you sign up with the CIA while I wasn't looking or something?"

Chad almost spat out his food. Recovering himself, he rolled his eyes and said, "What would the CIA want with me?"

Lies in the Sand

Realizing that Chad's answer was in fact a non-answer, Daniel pressed him. "I don't know – you tell me."

"Look, I'm just an underpaid college professor; do I look like I'm some kind of spy?" Chad asked, having completely stopped eating.

Another non-answer. Daniel said, "I'm not sure I'd know a spy if I saw one. Chad, are you a spy?"

Chad grinned and said, "Well, if I told you, I'd have to kill you now, wouldn't I?" He went back to his meal.

Annie laughed and they went on to other topics until they realized that it was after nine p.m. "Goodness, I've got to get back and get breakfast set up for tomorrow morning, guys, let's go."

They all stood. "What's for breakfast, anything good?" Chad asked, his eyes shining.

Daniel laughed. "After a huge seafood platter, extra hush puppies and three beers, how can you even think about food? There's something wrong with you, Buddy!"

Chad grinned and went back to asking Annie about the menu. It was clear to her that she was going to need extra breakfast food while this guy was staying.

Chapter 23

Daniel took a call from his boss the next morning with some unexpected news. A group of Chinese investors had become interested in the property and they were sending some representatives down to look it over. Daniel hung up, looked around his room and swallowed hard. Annie was not going to like this turn of events.

He went downstairs after the breakfast was all done and cleaned up. Annie was in her office/bedroom working on her computer. He knocked and stuck his head in. "Hey!"

She looked up and smiled at him. "Hey, yourself!"

"Uh…" he stammered… "you got a minute?"

"Sure, c'mon in." She removed a stack of papers from the only other chair in the room and he took a seat. "What's up? Hungry again already?" she asked with a big grin.

"No, that would be Chad, not me. I've got some news, Annie and you're not going to like it, I'm afraid…"

"What…?"

"My boss called and told me that a group of investors in China is interested in the property next door. They're sending some people down to check it out today. Nothing's final until after the auction, of course, but I wanted you to know."

Annie turned to him and hung her head. "Did he say what they wanted the property for, Daniel?"

He hesitated before answering. "Ron said that they're talking about the possibility of putting up some big condo units or huge houses. I'm sorry, Annie, I'm so sorry!" He reached out for her.

She drew back. "It's not your fault, Daniel, it's that new owner! He just wants to make as much money as possible on the sale." She hung her head. "And really, can you blame him for that? But that means that the price is going way up, doesn't it?" She looked to him for some kind of reassurance and comfort.

He nodded slowly. "Probably. Usually, it does."

Annie muttered something under her breath, turned back to her desk and went back to work. "Is that all?" she asked, shuffling papers on her desk.

Daniel could tell that this was no time for a long conversation. "Sure. Just wanted to let you know." He stood up and walked to the door. "See you later, okay?"

Annie grunted but didn't turn around.

That afternoon a team of Asian people, three men and one woman, showed up and knocked at the door of the *Sandy Bottom*. They asked for Daniel, who met them at the door and walked them around the house and down the beach to show them the property in question.

There was a flurry of Chinese conversation as he showed them around, but very little English. He did see a lot of head-nodding going on, though, so he assumed that they were pleased with what they saw. After some scouting around, they walked from the beach all the way through to the highway side of the lots, and then Daniel mentioned to them the odd reaction of compasses to this piece of land.

A hurried exchange followed, punctuated by some loud voices; Daniel wished that he knew at least a little Chinese so he could tell what was going on. About that time, Finis wandered up and stood beside Daniel on the pavement.

"Chinese investors, huh?" Finis asked nonchalantly as the visitors chatted away in their own language.

Daniel gave him a questioning look.

"Annie called me," Finis said. "Can I talk to them, do you think?"

"Uh... what is it you'd like to say to them?" Daniel asked, totally taken off guard by the request. Knowing how the old man felt about visitors, he was hesitant to put them through what Finis could dish out.

"Well, I reckon you'll find out if they listen, won't you?" Finis gave him a straight face.

"Well, I don't see any harm in it, I guess..." Daniel walked over to the one who appeared to be in charge and asked if they'd be willing to talk to Finis.

The man looked at Finis and asked, "Why he want to talk to us?"

Daniel said, "He's lived here all his life. He may have some interesting facts about the property that he wants to share with you." Daniel shrugged.

Another outbreak of Chinese exploded between the group and finally the leader said, "Okay, if he make it quick. We busy. Long drive back!" The group moved as one over toward the old man and bowed their heads respectfully.

Finis smiled, which totally threw Daniel for a loop. Finis looked at the man who appeared to be in charge. "Will you interpret or does everyone understand English?"

The lone woman answered, "We understand enough. You talk."

"Of course. My name is Finis and I live right over there." He pointed toward the road that led to his house. "I've lived here all my life and I know a lot about the history of the place."

The leader appeared to be growing impatient. "Yes, yes... I Mr. Chen. What you want to say?" He didn't offer to introduce the others.

Finis nodded at them. "Well, if you're interested in purchasing this property, I have some information that I'm sure you will all want to have." He leaned forward and spoke with a low voice. "This place is the home of evil spirits!"

The four Chinese talked quickly to each other, making sure that they had understood what the old man had said. The leader asked, "What you mean, evil spirits?"

Finis got a sober look on his face, glanced slowly around in both directions, leaned in again and said firmly, "I mean that demons live there!" He pointed toward the beach. "Have you seen what happens to a compass when you bring it near this place?"

Daniel shook his head. "No, I told them but I didn't show them."

Finis fished around in his pocket and took out an old, worn and slightly dented compass. He twitched his finger toward the four Chinese people for them to come closer. They gathered around. He looked each of them in the eye and then said, "Watch!" He flipped open the compass and the needle began to slowly swing to the left, and over to the right. Then it began to swing back and forth. Finis pointed toward it and said, "And the further you go in, the more it moves, until it spins around like crazy!" He made a small circle in the air with his finger and then threw up his hands.

All four of them gasped, covering their mouths. Finis leaned in and said, "The closer you get to where the spirits live, the worse it gets! Nobody around here will go onto this land because of all the evil spirits that live here! If you're going to buy it, you need to know this! This placed is cursed and anyone who tries to build here will pay with his life!"

This time the flurry of Chinese was loud and long. While they talked they moved their hands about in dramatic gestures. Daniel could tell that this whole thing was spinning out of control, but what could he do?

Finis looked at Daniel, grinned, then turned to the Chinese and said, "If you want to take my compass and walk in further, then here," he said, holding it out to them. "See for yourself. But me, I ain't steppin' foot off this pavement to go onto that cursed land!" The old man looked very afraid.

They all four at once held up their hands and waved them around in the universal sign for 'no way!'. Finally, the group turned to Finis. The woman spoke. "You say place is home of evil spirits. How you know this?" She appeared to be the skeptic of the group.

Finis got a sad look on his face. "My grandmother died because of the curse; my family has passed down the stories of shipwrecks out there, and how lots of people have died after being on that very land, and I myself have seen it kill animals. I never go onto that land myself. Never!" He shook his head twice.

"Died?!!" one of the others squeaked. "People die?" He looked terrified.

Finis nodded slowly. "My great-great grandfather called the evil spirits 'mogwai,' whatever that means... And he made all of his descendants swear to keep off the land, no matter what!"

The woman gasped. "*Mogwai*? That Chinese word! Mean evil monster, ghost, very bad spirit!"

Finis looked surprised. "Chinese? Mogwai is a Chinese word? How about that! Maybe he learned it from that Chinese boat that was shipwrecked out there," he said, pointing toward the ocean. "He was a life-saver and he said that the only sailor who they recovered alive from the wreck kept saying the word 'mogwai!' over and over. But then the sailor died, so grandpa never found out what the word meant..." He looked at them innocently and shrugged.

"Chinese sailor died?" Mr. Chen asked.

Finis nodded and said, "A whole shipload of them!"

Daniel and Finis stood back as a long conversation in Chinese ensued. The two of them kept quiet with their hands in their pockets, trying to look like they didn't understand what was going on. But the body language was pretty easy to read, and they could see clearly; it looked like two for, two against.

Finis spoke up. "Now, I can take you down to see our historian, Pete at the Rusty Anchor Bar, down the road apiece, he's the man who owns the bar and he has heard all the stories that have been told. He can tell you much more about the mogwai than me, all I know is what's been passed down from my elders."

They quickly agreed to go and talk to Pete. Finis said, "Daniel, you ride with them. I'll take my truck." Daniel agreed and the two of them stepped away from the chattering group for a moment of privacy.

"What was that about?" Daniel whispered.

"What?" Finis asked, wide eyed.

"You old coot! You know just what I'm talking about! Where did you come up with all of that baloney about the evil spirits?"

Finis grinned. "Annie called and she was all upset about Chinese investors building condos on the lot. I thought about it and figured I'd come over and help out."

"You made all that stuff up?" Daniel asked.

Finis nodded slightly.

"The dead animals even? What about the 'mogwai' thing? Where'd you come up with that?"

"Google," Finis deadpanned. "Oh, and I called ahead and told Pete what I was doing, and he said he'll finish 'em up for us." Finis turned and walked toward home, waving over his shoulder. "See you at the Rusty Anchor," he called out.

Daniel stared at the old man's back as Finis sauntered away, hands in his pockets, whistling some tune. Daniel grinned, then put a serious look on his face and turned back to the Chinese group. He gathered them up and they walked slowly back to the *Sandy Bottom*; the ones who weren't chattering were on their phones either calling or searching for information. He stood, waiting for them to finish up.

After a long discussion, they all got in the car and headed for the *Rusty Anchor* shortly afterward. Finis had beaten them there and had finished one beer already. He grinned and waved them in, all hospitality and friendliness. "Mr. Chen and associates, this is Pete, my friend. He's owned this bar for forty years, and he's heard all of the stories about the land – and the mogwai, too – right Pete?"

Pete got a confused look on his face. Finis said, "You know, Pete, the *mogwai* – the evil spirits that haunt that place!"

Pete quickly recovered. "Sure have! Those mog-wi are some scary things! Nice to meet you, folks, please come in and take a seat at the bar. Let me serve you a free drink – complimentary – and then I will tell you all about it." He reached for a pitcher of drinks on ice that he'd already made up and began to pour out four good-sized glasses before the visitors even had a chance to answer. "This is a local drink – you will like it very much! Maybe you have a drink like this?" He passed them out quickly.

Finis stepped behind the bar, refilled his beer glass and poured a beer for Daniel, who looked over at the mixed drink and said, "Can't I have one of those?"

Finis shook his head slightly and whispered. "You'll have to drive them back to a hotel probably." He nodded toward the pitcher. "That's some really smooth local moonshine mixed with a little orange juice. Pete only makes up a batch every once in a while; he calls the drink a 'Florida Serial Killer.' You'll see why."

The four well-dressed visitors sipped on their drinks hesitantly. Then they looked at one another, smiled and nodded. They settled back to listen as Pete began to spin his tales, complete with dramatic gestures. His tenure as a bartender had made him quite the accomplished entertainer. They gasped, nodded, and cringed as Pete told them tales of shipwrecks, mutilations and disappearances all due to the 'mogwai.' Daniel stood spellbound and listened to the stories. He turned to Finis, who just grinned and nodded.

After one more round of drinks, the visitors were somewhere between giddy and terrified. And by then they loved Pete, who catered to them in every way possible. When they excused themselves to walk over by the door and have a private discussion, Pete looked to Finis and Daniel. "How'd I do?" he asked quietly, wiping the bar.

Lies in the Sand

"Well, I'll never buy that land!" Daniel said. "In fact, I don't ever want to walk on it again!"

Pete rolled his eyes. "That was just a bunch of Outer Banks ghost stories all rolled into one! And I'm pretty sure that none of 'em are true!"

Daniel laughed softly. "You had me going, Pete!"

Pete nodded. "Anything for Annie! You get any more idiots wantin' to build condos or gift shops there, you just send 'em down to me. Me and Finis will take care of them, huh, Finis?"

Finis burped loudly, patted his belly and said, "Like you said, anything for Annie!"

Daniel drove for the giddy group, helped the visitors secure lodging nearby for the night, pointed them toward a good restaurant and then Finis offered to drive him back to Annie's place. They couldn't help noticing that the Chinese woman was getting really friendly with one of her cohorts. And the other two fellows tried hard to stand up straight as they checked in, but both looked a little like branches blowing in the wind. Daniel figured they might not make it anywhere for dinner tonight.

Finis laughed as they drove back. "I guess some things are good for international trade, and some things not-so-much!" He slapped the steering wheel and laughed again.

Daniel was beginning to get a real 'read' on Finis, so he thought this might be a good time to be bold and ask him something that he'd been wondering about. "Say, Finis," he said, hesitated to see what kind of a reaction that breach of propriety brought, then went on when he didn't get hit or cussed out. "Do you feel like telling me how you got your first name, Finis, it's very unusual. Don't think I've ever heard it before…"

Finis smiled and kept his eyes on the road. "I reckon I could do that. My mamma was part French, and she spoke some French that'd been passed down to her from my grandmother, who was shipwrecked here when she was a girl. Mamma had a bunch of babies before me, and by the time she had me, she looked at my father and said, 'fin-eee', which is French for 'finished' and she decided to name me that. My father wouldn't have it pronounced in

Lies in the Sand

French 'cause he said it sounded like a girl's name, so he called me Fi-ness, which I reckon had a more manly sound to him. Me, I don't see the difference, but after all these years, I've got used to it."

Daniel laughed out loud. "So, she was done with babies, huh?" He made a slashing motion with his hand.

Finis nodded. "Yep. No more after me. And Daniel..."

"Uh-huh?"

The old man returned to his rough persona. "If you ever tell that story to anybody, I'll cut your tongue out. It's mine to tell to whoever I please, not yours. You got that?"

"Absolutely, Mr. Turnbull. Your secret's safe with me!"

Finis grunted and nodded.

Lies in the Sand

Chapter 24

The following morning Chad was on the phone for hours. The single woman went off to do some shopping after she checked out, so that left Annie and Daniel alone together after breakfast. They sat on the porch, walked on the beach, and tried not to talk about the property.

She discovered that he was a Star Wars nut. So was she. Talking about how they loved the latest movie took them at least an hour, and when they went into theories about who was so-and-so's parents and who had to die next for the saga to continue, the conversation got pretty out-there.

"Okay, we'll agree to disagree, then," Daniel said, laughing, as they walked toward the back porch. "But when the next movie comes out, I'll be vindicated, I'm sure of it!"

Annie laughed so hard that she snorted. He thought that was adorable, too. She took his arm as they walked and said, "You want to put some money on that?" She smiled innocently.

He looked down at her hand wrapped around his upper arm. It was all he could do to keep from kissing her. She was so beautiful, so smart, so wickedly funny… He cleared his throat and said. "How about a hundred?"

She grinned. "You're on. Get ready to pay up in a couple of years, Mr. Know-it-all!"

Terry was watching them from inside. She slapped the side of her leg with her hand and hooted. He would be just what Annie needed! She was going to have to do some maneuvering of her own, just to get this thing kickstarted before Daniel had to leave.

"Hey, you two, how about some ham sandwiches for lunch?" she asked when they came inside, still laughing.

Daniel looked up. "I thought this was a Bed and Breakfast, not three-square meals a day!" He looked between the two ladies.

Annie laughed. "Well, we'll make an exception this time. Daniel, go up and see if Chad wants to join us for lunch, why don't you?"

"Sure, but I don't think Chad has ever turned down food," he said and bounded up the stairs.

Annie turned to Terry. "We just had this big, long Star Wars discussion," she said giddily, as she got out some plates, napkins and silverware. "That dufus thinks he knows all about stuff that hasn't even been written yet!" she added, laughing. "That'll be an easy hundred bucks I'll take off him when the next movie comes out!" She began to hum as she worked.

Yep. She's gone. Terry grinned and put out the sandwiches, some potato salad and a few other items.

When the boys came and sat at the table, Terry asked, "So, what have you discovered, Chad? What's the big mysterious deal with the land next door?"

Chad was already busy stuffing his face so Daniel answered. "He's playing his cards close to the chest, Terry. I personally think that he's some kind of CIA spy and that he believes there's a UFO buried out there…"

Chad choked and bits of sandwich went flying. He wiped his mouth and said, "Sorry… I just wasn't ready for that one!" He cleared his throat and took a drink. "Actually, Terry, I'm not sure what's out there. But one of my geology buddies from Washington is coming down, bringing some more sensitive equipment, to help me explore this phenomenon." He turned to Annie. "Could he stay here for a few days, Annie? He's an older guy, doesn't smoke, nice fellow?"

She nodded. "Of course. You two are my only guests right now and I don't have any more reservations for another week or so. Let me see: you're in Room 3, I'll put your friend in Room 1, it's empty now. Tell him to come on, it's fine and we'll be glad to have him. I may have to give ya'll the group rate if this keeps going!"

"Alright!" Chad said, grabbing what was left of his sandwich. "Hey, Terry, how much would it cost me to get another one of these?" he asked, holding out the remainder. "This is the best ham sandwich I've ever had!" He bit down with vigor.

"Oh, I'll bet you say that to all the sandwich makers, Chad," she said sarcastically, batting her eyelashes at him. "Will one more be enough, Sir?" she asked.

He appeared to think about it before saying, "Yeah, I believe one more will do it!"

Annie looked at Terry. "Weighs the same as he did in college. Don't ask." She shook her head. Terry rolled her eyes and got up to make his sandwich.

After finishing up everything on the table, Chad leaned back and patted his stomach. "That ought to hold me for a few hours," he said.

"...or a few days," Terry muttered under her breath.

"When will you be able to tell us something, Chad?" Annie asked.

He thought about it. "Well, after Frank gets here and we have a day or two to go over our findings, maybe then."

"Well, I tell you what, then," Annie said. "I'll provide breakfast and lunch for Daniel and you mad scientists during your stay and that way you won't have to stop what you're doing and go out for lunch. But I draw the line at dinners – that ain't gonna happen, fellas!" she said, pointing at them and raising an eyebrow.

"Sounds like a good deal to me," Chad answered. "We'll just have to take you two ladies out for dinner at night." He grinned at Terry, who ignored him and stood up to clean the table. She figured that a man like that was only interested in the food she could make for him and she certainly didn't want to encourage *that*.

That afternoon late, Frank arrived and moved in. His presence was warm and fatherly, something Annie loved. After only a few hours and a meal together, the five of them began to feel like a small family, bonded by the mystery of the property with the so-called curse.

After dinner, the girls went back. Daniel took Chad and Frank to meet Pete at the *Rusty Anchor*, and it was well past midnight before they staggered back in, slapping each other on the back and laughing. Annie peeked out from her downstairs bedroom, shook her head and went back to bed.

Chapter 25

Except for Chad's, appetites were a bit off the next morning.

"So, how'd y'all like Pete?" Annie asked, refilling coffee cups the next morning. "You boys have a good time?"

Frank looked happy at being called a boy and said, "Pete is the kind of man who was born to be a bartender! And he told us this long story about how he met his girlfriend Maggie; her husband had disappeared, then the mafia and the FBI came down and got involved – it was quite a tale!"

Annie nodded. "I've heard that story. Seems like every time he tells it, it changes a little bit. I don't believe half of it, it's just too bizarre... people disappearing without a trace and all that." She waved her hand. "I think he made most of it up."

Finis walked in about that time, and all heads turned toward him.

"Come on in, Finis, let me pour you some coffee!" Annie said, calling him over. He sat down at the long table and she introduced the two men that he hadn't met yet.

Chad stuck out his hand and said, "Nice to meet you, Finis." Daniel did a double take; Chad had called the old codger by his first name and he'd only just met him! *This was not going to go well...* Daniel thought. But Finis nodded, shook his hand and smiled – smiled!

Frank extended his hand as well. "Heard a lot about you, Finis, you're a bit of a legend around here! I'd love to talk to you about the history of this island if you've got time."

Finis shook Frank's hand and nodded. "Always time for Annie's friends," he said, and cast a sideways glance at Daniel, who was sitting there with his mouth hanging open. "Shut your trap, boy, or you'll ketch flies," he said, and reached for his coffee. Daniel closed his mouth. Finis grinned. Annie turned away and tried to hide her smile.

"We were just talking about the mystery of the property next door," Frank said.

"Ain't no mystery! It's a curse," Finis said, as if no other explanation was anywhere near making sense.

"Yes, well..." Frank continued, "Chad and I are studying the geological aspect of it – that is to say, the rocks and minerals involved."

Finis looked a bit put-out. "I know what geology is, Frank. Been to school, you know."

Frank quickly said, "Sorry, of course you do. And you'll be interested to know that we've found some strange properties to the soil in certain areas of that plot."

"No surprise there," Finis said, sipping his coffee. "Coulda told ya'll that forty years ago."

"Right...." Chad put in. "And Finis, I'd like to hear what you know about this curse, if you don't mind telling me."

Finis looked questioningly at Annie. She nodded. "They're good people, Finis, and none of them will be making any money or anything off of this," she said.

Studying something across the room, Finis thought about it for a few moments. "Alright. But if you fellas think that you're gonna make a fool out of this old country boy, then I want to be there to see the look on your faces when you find out I was right all along." He grinned and proceeded to tell them the same things he'd told Daniel, together with Pete's additional details.

Chad raised his eyebrows, barely containing a snarky comment, but Frank nodded seriously as Finis told the tale. After he was all done, Frank said, "Finis, how much of this do you think is really true?"

"Well, I do believe that there's some kind of treasure buried there and that Blackbeard buried it. But you better not mention the word *treasure* outside this room, or we'll have all kinds of greedy idiots with metal detectors coming down here!" He gave them a severe look and both men nodded. "And the part about the curse, well, I might think that was kind of built-up over the years maybe, except for the compass thing. There's something real weird about it; that's not a natural occurrence, you have to admit," Finis said, looking pointedly at Chad.

Chad nodded. "Absolutely. Totally agree with you there!" His attempt to mollify the old man was met with a look that said, 'You ain't dealin' with no fool here, youngun'. Chad looked away.

Frank stepped in. "Yes, you're right about that, Finis. Let me ask you this, have you ever explored the property, even as a boy?"

Finis shook his head. "Nope. My father told me about how his mother died when he did that as a boy, and I'm no genius, but I do not believe in tempting fate. My grandpa told me the same thing, and he made a believer out of me."

"What kind of man was your grandfather?" Frank asked.

Finis grabbed his coffee cup with both hands and leaned back in his chair. "He was one tough son-of-a-gun, you can bet your britches on that!" he said, smiling. "My mamma saw him wrestle men twice his weight and take 'em down. He was wiry, but tall, and people all around here respected him. He was good to his family and good to his community. He was one of the surfmen that worked for the National Life Saving Service back in the day, and in my book, that made him a real hero!"

Annie nodded. "So true!"

"And besides," Finis said, "I never knew him to say anything bad about anybody or to tell a lie." He looked straight at Chad. "If he told you something, you could believe it! So... I believe it." Finis went on to tell them stories about how his grandfather and great-grandfather had saved the lives of many people during awful shipwrecks caused by storms, and how the Surfmen's motto, 'You have to go out, but you don't have to come back,' showed the kind of men they were.

"Wow!" Daniel said. "I never knew about all that!"

Finis said, "Take a trip down the road a little way and visit the Chicamacomico Life Saving Station Museum, son, and you'll see just what kind of heroes they were!"

Daniel nodded and said that he'd do that as soon as he could. They sat around the table discussing island history and folklore, and managed to keep away from the subject of the curse and the mystery. Soon Finis stood up and said, "Well, all ya'll professionals might not have anything to do, but I've got chores at home that need tendin' to, so I'm headed home. Thanks for the coffee, Annie, you're a good girl." He nodded and walked over to the door.

"Bye, Mr. Turnbull, Sir," Daniel called out.

Finis waved over his shoulder without turning around or saying a word, and walked out the door.

"Mr. Turnbull, *Sir*?" Chad asked with a questioning look on his face.

Annie said, "It's a long story, guys, but basically it's just Finis' way of seeing what kind of man Daniel is."

"Why didn't you tell me that in the first place?" Daniel asked. "That it was some kind of test?"

Annie smiled and shrugged. "I had my reasons. And by the way, you're doing better than expected."

Chad snorted, Terry laughed, and Daniel looked confused. Frank tried hard to suppress a smile in sympathy. They all got up and headed their separate ways.

Chapter 26

That afternoon Daniel received a call from the representatives of the Chinese group. They requested a meeting with him and agreed to meet him at the *Rusty Anchor*. Pete was happy to see them again and ready to spin more tales, but they declined any more drinks or stories and stuck with coffee as they talked.

"So, Mr. Chen, what did all of you think of the property?" "Daniel asked. "Does it look like something that your investors would be interested in?"

Mr. Chen looked troubled and shook his head. "Talked on phone with China this morning. Our employer a very religious man, believe in spirits. We told him stories of Pete, and he become frightened. He say we look for different property, don't want get involved with mogwai or bad things happen to us if we build."

The woman spoke up. "He very rich but backward in some ways." The other three looked at her in surprise. She nodded and said. "This true. You know it true!" And sipped her coffee. The men squirmed a bit and then nodded reluctantly.

Mr. Chen said, "So we go now to place called Nag's Head to look at property number two. Better." He looked at Daniel. "What does word 'nag' mean? No translation make us understand!"

Daniel laughed. "It's another word for horse."

The four of them looked even more confused. "Horse's head is name of town?" The woman asked.

"Annie told me that they named it 'Nag's Head' because they used to hang a lantern around the horse's neck and walk it up and down the beach on dark nights. That way ships carrying illegal goods would know where it was safe to come ashore."

The group looked at Daniel and then at one another in confusion.

"Doesn't matter," Daniel said, waving his hand. "Yes, 'Nag's Head' is the name of a town north of here on the Outer Banks."

"Okay," Mr. Chen said. "We want to thank you for time you spend with us. You nice man. Sorry deal not work out." The other three nodded. They finished their coffee, got into their car, and headed north.

Pete looked at Daniel. "Well? Did it work? Are they buying the property?"

Daniel laughed and shook his head. "I believe that once the word gets out in China, nobody from there will ever buy anything on the Outer Banks again!"

They high-fived each other and Pete bought him a beer.

Frank and Chad had made some calls later that day, and then informed Annie that some additional people were coming down from Washington the following day. The two of them offered to double-up to make an additional room available, and Daniel offered to sleep on the sofa downstairs if it came to that. It would be tight, but they would be able to handle the crowd. Annie loved the over-full booking, but all those breakfasts and lunches would be a lot of extra work. Terry agreed to come full-time and help out with meals, cleaning and what not.

Chapter 27

Frank's phone call must have caused a stir, because late the following morning the two men and two women 'experts' arrived. They introduced themselves as geologists working with the Smithsonian Institute. The women agreed to share Room 2, but the men wouldn't even consider that. So all four upstairs rooms were full and Daniel would be losing his room and sleeping on the sofa. They settled in quickly and then got to work out in the field and also on their phones.

Daniel took a call from his boss, Ron Bentley, who was still being harassed by Felix Benefield to get on with the auction. They had agreed not to inform the easily-irritated Felix of the geological teams working on his property, and had put him off with the 'still tracking down the little glitch in the title work' excuse. And that part was true, because the Register of Deed's office in Manteo still hadn't gotten back to Daniel.

But Felix wasn't buying it; his attorney told him that a title search had been done and title insurance purchased, so it was a done deal and there was no need for a delay. He pitched a phone-fit and demanded Ron get it done. Daniel agreed to try to speed the scientists along, if possible.

Finis was watching the activity on the property – from a distance – and was always ready to walk over to Annie's and give the experts advice on how to do their job. They all did their best to placate him respectfully as long as he stayed out of their way.

After lunch, the geologists got back to work; Daniel caught up with Annie and they sat out on the back porch together. The weather continued to be sunny and pleasant, if a bit on the chilly side when you were out in the wind. Perfect spring beach weather!

Lies in the Sand

"I've been here a week today, Annie, and my boss Ron let me know that we had to get this thing sewed up fast; the Seller is threatening to sue us over the delay... We haven't informed him that the geologists are working there because we knew that he'd throw a fit!"

"Ah! The old 'better to get forgiveness than permission' approach, huh?" she said.

He nodded. "I don't see that they'll damage anything, and they'll be out of here soon, they said, but this seller - he's not an easy one to work with."

Annie looked troubled and said, "Do the scientists know about this?"

Daniel nodded. "Yes, I told them that they needed to hurry. But they didn't seem particularly concerned, or even interested, for that matter. You know how nerds are... don't bother them with mundane details!"

Annie laughed. "Daniel, I have to admit, I'm going to hate to see you go," she said shyly, not looking at him. "Having you here has made this whole thing like an adventure – a lot of extra work, but a lot of fun. No matter how the sale of the property goes, I do hope that you'll be coming back to visit us again." She still couldn't look at him.

He reached over and put his hand on top of hers. "You better believe it, Annie. I've come to love this place – and the people here." He squeezed her hand and she turned toward him smiling. "Especially my hostess."

She raised one eyebrow and looked at him oddly.

"Just sayin'", he said, looking out at the water.

Soon they saw the whole gang of scientists walking back toward the house. "Looks like they're making it a short day," he said. They all came up, chatting excitedly, but suddenly went silent when they saw the two of them sitting on the porch.

"What? Have you found some kind of government secret that we can't know about?" Daniel teased. They all looked at each other.

Chad said, "You and your conspiracy theories, Daniel! It's just a lot of technobabble and we didn't want to talk over your heads, that's all! But we do need to use the main room downstairs as a conference room for a while, if you would give us the privacy."

Annie nodded. "Sure, I need to go shopping anyway because Chad's eating me out of house and home. C'mon Daniel, you go with me. I'll take you over to Chicamacomico and let Dinah and John show you around. You'll learn all about how the surfmen worked and lived."

Chad said, "Oh, and Annie, we have one more person coming in tomorrow…"

"To stay here? Where will I put them?" she asked.

Chad smiled. "Not to worry, we'll work something out, I promise!"

"If you say so," Annie said, shaking her head. They grabbed their things and took off in Daniel's car. The gang of scientists got busy setting up the large table and computers even before they got out the door.

Annie looked back as they drove away. "I wonder what's got them so excited, and who this new person is?" she said.

Daniel shrugged. "Maybe they discovered a new kind of mineral, or they found a buried alien spaceship down there with their fancy ground radar," he teased.

She swatted him on the shoulder. "Right, sure! Then they'll build a big government 'Area-51' base here and throw the rest of us off the island!" She laughed out loud. "I love how you make me laugh, Daniel!"

Well, that's a start… he thought.

Lies in the Sand

Chapter 28

Annie took Daniel to the Chicamacomico Life Saving Station Museum in Rodanthe on their way to the store. Looking from the outside, he was not very impressed; it seemed to be just another large cottage, like so many other old places along the beach. But once they got inside, it was another matter!

They were given a special tour that included the background, training, and duties of the seven or so Surfmen who lived and worked there at one time. These brave men faced daily training that was so intensive that few could handle it, so it took a special kind of man to be a Surfman. They lived there full-time during the stormy season, were paid little and given no retirement benefits when they got old. Making a living while they were off duty was their own problem, and many of them had families.

Now owned by the Coast Guard, Annie said that the Chicamacomico Museum is perhaps the most overlooked tourist attraction on the Outer Banks. Once a person goes there, their views of life on those shores in those days will change forever. And their definition of a 'hero' is changed forever.

Daniel learned of the historic rescue of the British Tanker *Mirlo* in 1918. Chicamacomico Station personnel saved forty-two crew members of that ship. The tanker had been torpedoed and was on fire, lying about five miles out to sea. The surfmen spotted the smoke and fire and determined to go out to help if they could.

Among the burning wreckage and heavy seas were a few lifeboats containing survivors. One boat was located which held the captain and sixteen of his men. Chicamacomico's Captain Midgett directed it to a specific spot nearby to wait for them, because he was not sure that their lifeboat would survive the heavy surf on its way to the beach with untrained men at the helm. He would have his own men bring them to safety.

The surfmen then spotted an upturned lifeboat among the floating wreckage, with six men clinging to it for dear life. Those unfortunate men all had burns to some degree, but because they had at times dived under the water to save themselves from being burned alive, they'd managed to survive. These men didn't know anything about where the other lifeboats were or even if anyone else had survived. Captain Midgett rescued those men in his own boat and then set out to locate the others.

After that, Captain Midgett ordered his men to search in the vicinity of the fire for more survivors. Those brave lifesavers, not sparing their own lives, headed back into the great clouds of smoke and fire rising from the burning gas and oil. No more men were found among the wreckage, but they learned that there was yet another lifeboat, a third one, that was missing. Eventually they located the third lifeboat about nine miles south of the station, containing nineteen men. They pulled alongside them and then took them to where the first boat had been told to wait.

As it grew dark, Captain Midgett decided it was time to make a landing. He anchored the two lifeboats about six hundred yards from shore, and then transferred the rescued men to his station boat, leaving his own men to bring the lifeboats ashore in those dangerous conditions. The Surfmen's rigorous, intense training paid off, and they were able to all come ashore safely.

The survivors and crew were taken from their beach landing back to Chicamacomico Station by two teams of horses, where they were given needed medical aid, dry clothing and food, as well as a place to sleep. Twelve years later, in 1930, Captain Midgett and his crew received The Grand Cross from Great Britain (one of their highest honors given) for their heroism.

This was just one example of the brave deeds of the Life Saving Service heroes, and that same kind of heroism was repeated many times up and down the Atlantic Coast while they were guarding those shores. These brave men had an unheard-of ***99% success rate*** for the rescues they performed during their service. In 1915, the Life Saving Service was merged with the U.S. Revenue Cutter Service to form the U.S. Coast Guard.

Daniel was especially moved by what he saw when he observed the size of the wooden boats those men went out in before gas motors came along – sixteen footers that many times would have to be rowed manually through three rough sets of breakers and heavy seas during a hurricane to rescue stranded ship's personnel.

After thanking the station personnel for his tour, he spent the rest of the trip discussing with Annie the bravery of those men – heroes that he'd never even heard of before. He determined to go back to Raleigh and tell all of his 'landlubber' friends and relatives about his experience and encourage them to take the tour as well!

Lies in the Sand

Chapter 29

When Annie and Daniel arrived back at the B&B, they noticed that a different car had been parked hastily in the driveway, and there seemed to be a loud ruckus going on inside. They hurried in with the groceries and saw a man standing in the hallway, both doors to the conference room now flung open, waving his arms around and shouting at Chad and the other scientists.

"I want all of you off my property this minute!" he demanded. "I mean it – now!" He ranted and raved a little more and appeared to be highly volatile.

Annie walked up to him and gently touched his arm to get his attention. "Excuse me, Sir, I don't know who you are, but this happens to be *my property* that you're standing on right now. Would you please calm down so we can discuss this?" She smiled at him in an understanding way, but he would have none of it.

He glared at her. "I don't care who you are or what you own, lady, I want you to call the police right now!" He thumped his chest. "I'm Felix Benefield! These people have been trespassing on my property and I want all of 'em locked up!"

Annie looked over at the scientists, who didn't seem particularly concerned. One of them was on the phone and the others just stood there with their arms crossed, letting the guy vent.

"What property are we talking about?" Daniel asked as he walked up to the man.

"Who are you?" Felix spat back.

"I'm Daniel Marcus and I'm here on business for my company."

Lies in the Sand

"Are you the idiot from the auction house who keeps putting off the sale? What are you trying to do, you fool, ruin me? That property *is mine*, and I want it sold – now!" He shook his finger in Daniel's face. Daniel took a step back.

Annie said, "Please, Mr. Benefield, calm down. We'll get this all worked out. How do you know that these people have been on your property?"

Felix blustered. "Well, when I saw all these cars, I walked down to take a look. It's clear that *somebody's* been digging around out there and it must be these people, look at those maps spread around! And all that equipment laying in your backyard tells me everything I need to know! This is an outrage!"

Daniel spoke up. "Do you have any witnesses who can place these people on your property?"

Felix walked over, invading Daniel's personal space, and exploded. "I don't have to put up with this crap, especially from you! You're supposed to be working for me!" He turned and pointed at the scientists. "And all of you are trespassers! I'm calling the cops, right now!" He stormed out the front door, slamming it shut and got right on his cell phone. He screamed into the phone as he paced up and down the porch.

"Uh... what do we do now?" Annie asked, looking around.

Frank got off the phone and spoke up. "Not to worry, it's all being handled." The others chatted quietly with Frank and then nodded in an agreeable way and went back to their computers. Frank smiled at her and got back to work himself.

Annie shook her head; they all seemed so calm, especially when you realized that they had in fact been trespassing without permission... "Come on, Daniel, let's put this food away," Annie said, heading into the kitchen. When they got inside, she shut the door, which normally remained open all day and night.

"Daniel, what in the world is this about?" she demanded, her hands on her hips.

Lies in the Sand

He shrugged. "I guess that's the crazy Seller that my boss warned me about, but he didn't say anything about the guy actually coming here... As far as the nerds go, I have no idea. Wait, let's call Chad in here." He went to the door, walked into the great room and drug Chad back into the kitchen.

Daniel used his firm voice. "Spill it, Chad! This is no longer a little geology research project, that's guy's out there calling the police! What's up?" He crossed his arms, and Annie backed him up by standing beside him crossing her arms as well.

"Uh...can we sit down?" Chad asked, motioning toward the small table in the middle of the large kitchen.

"Okay," Annie said, "but you better talk fast and tell us something good, because that guy looks violent and he's getting the police involved!" She pointed toward Felix pacing on the porch as he yelled into the phone. They all took a seat.

"How long will it take the police to get here?" Chad asked.

She thought for a moment. "Well, there's a Police Department in Buxton, and they'll be at least twenty minutes, probably longer because it's not an emergency. And they will probably be in touch with the Dare County Sheriff's Department in Manteo, which is maybe thirty minutes away. Now keep in mind that in the Outer Banks, unless it's an emergency, they're not going to send anybody out immediately, sirens blaring. They handle kooks like him on the phone all the time, I'm sure."

Chad nodded. "Okay, that should be enough time," he said.

"For what?" Daniel asked.

Chad looked a little embarrassed, cleared his throat and said, "Well, Frank called in these new people and they *are* scientists, but they don't work for the Smithsonian only, they work for a lot of government agencies. And some of those agencies have a lot of legal and political power. I'm sure that right now, in Washington, somebody is on the phone with the local Police and the Dare County Sheriff, explaining what needs to be done..."

Annie and Daniel looked at one another and then at Chad. "What exactly is going on here, Chad?" Annie demanded. "You have to tell us the truth because we're in this up to our necks, too!" She jammed her pointer finger on the table top a few times for emphasis.

He squirmed in his seat. "I can't go into the details, but the government has sent them here to explore the, uh, 'magnetic phenomenon' in the soil. I'm pretty sure that they think there's something big buried under there, but without excavation, they can't be sure exactly what…"

"Something buried? Out there? So, they're going to dig up the place?" Annie asked. "Oh, no, I've got guests coming next week!"

Chad shook his head. "Trust me, Annie, this will all be done and over with by then. They've already called in for the heavy equipment, and when this bunch is done, you'll never know anyone has been there."

Annie looked at Daniel. "He's scaring me, Daniel."

Daniel nodded. "Me, too!" He turned toward Chad. "So, what do we do now?"

Chad shook his head. "Nothing. Like I said, it'll all be over soon, and with so little fuss and hubbub that nobody will notice, I imagine."

"I don't know," Annie said. "The locals here are pretty nosey and a bunch of strangers coming in with heavy equipment will get them all fired up…"

"Trust me," Chad said. "It'll be fine." He stood up. "Now I need to get back to work. And if it's alright with you, I'll leave the kitchen door closed and ask the two of you to stay out of our conference room. We'll close the big pocket doors leading into the hall and ask that you keep everyone else please."

"I'm not sure I like this…" Annie said.

Chad shook his head. "Not to worry, Annie, I've been assure that you'll be generously compensated for being put-out like this. *Generously.*" He smiled and headed out of the kitchen and back to work, carefully closing the door behind him.

Lies in the Sand

Annie and Daniel looked at one another, speechless. They put the groceries away and discussed the crazy situation they were in as calmly as possible. Daniel suggested that all the men get together and physically remove Felix from the premises, but Annie thought that might get out of control fast. Then they heard even louder shouting from the front porch. It sounded like Felix was about to go postal, so they went out there together to calm him down.

As they opened the front door and walked out, Felix spun around toward them. "You two stay away from me, the police are coming!" he shouted, pointing at them. "I'm on the phone with my lawyer and I'm going to sue everybody involved in this! You're about to lose your house, lady," he said and went back to his phone call.

Annie looked at Daniel with big eyes; this was quickly spinning out of control. Daniel waited until Felix hung up and then walked over to him. "Now wait a minute, Mr. Benefield, none of this is her fault! And you can't go threatening her like that, you've got no reason – "

Felix drew back his fist and took a swing at Daniel, who ducked just in time. Before the scuffle could turn more violent, a police car with sirens blaring pulled up into the yard and slammed on its brakes, skidding on the gravel. That drew everyone's attention quickly. Two officers with guns hopped out, guns drawn.

Felix straightened up and put his arms down. "Now you'll see!" he shouted. "Officers, these people are trespassing and damaging my property! Arrest all of them, now!"

The two policemen slowly walked up onto the porch, guns still out. "Hey, Annie!" one of them said and nodded toward her.

"Hey, Mike, hey Phil," she said, nodding at them.

The officer name Mike said, "Is this guy causing you problems?"

"What! Me?" Felix hollered.

Annie nodded. "I asked him to leave my property and he refused. He's been threatening all of us and just now he took a swing at my friend Daniel here."

"Why, you lying –" Felix said, turning angrily toward Annie with his fists coming up. Daniel quickly stepped in between them and then Phil grabbed Felix's hands and jerked them behind his back, holding him firmly.

Felix pivoted his head. "I'm not the person you need to arrest, these other people are!" he spat. "Take your hands off me now, or I'll sue you!"

Officer Mike walked over and zip-tied Felix's hands behind his back as Phil held him still. "Looks to me like he's high on something, wouldn't you agree?" Mike said. "Annie, do you want to press charges of trespassing and causing a public disturbance against this person?"

"Absolutely," she said, nodding and crossing her arms.

He turned to Daniel. "And you, sir, would you like to press charges for assault? We witnessed his attack on you as we drove up." He gave Daniel a half-smile.

"You bet," Daniel said. "Throw the book at him!"

"Come with us, sir," Phil said, turning Felix toward the steps and forcing him toward the car. "We don't take kindly to your type here on Hatteras Island, this is a peaceful place." It all happened so fast that Felix looked, for once, speechless. But he recovered quickly and fought Phil every step of the way, spouting threats and curses.

As Felix was being loaded into the cruiser, the Dare County Sheriff drove up. He chatted briefly with Phil outside the vehicle, then walked up on the porch and said, "Hey, Annie."

"Hey, David," she said, grinning.

The Sheriff looked at the policeman still on the porch. "You got this handled then, Mike?"

He nodded. "Everything's nicely tied up," he said with a grin as he glanced toward Felix screaming and kicking the door in the back seat of the cruiser. "We got the call and were nearby, so we hurried over here. We're locking him up for trespassing, public disturbance and assault. And he's getting a drug test, too!"

"Alright, then, I'll just follow you down to the station. We may need to move him to the Manteo jail after that, just so you know."

"You're welcome to him, Dave," the policeman said. "We'll meet you at the station." He turned toward Annie and Daniel. "Don't worry about a thing. He's clearly in the wrong here and we're going to keep him locked up because he's obviously violent and a threat to you." He cocked his head and thought for a moment. "He might even be mentally deranged and need to be hospitalized for examination..." he looked toward the sheriff, who grinned and lifted one shoulder. The officer touched the brim of his cap. "Take care, ya'll." He went to the car and the two policemen drove away with the man in the back seat still shouting.

The Sheriff took them aside. "Now I can't go into the details, but you can be sure that you won't have any more trouble from that one," he said, nodding toward the car that was leaving.

"Thanks, David," Annie said, and patted him on the arm. "He had me a bit scared there for a few minutes!"

"I'm just glad the psycho didn't have a gun!" Daniel added, nodding.

Sheriff Dave puckered lips lips and moved his mouth around, then said, "Well, we'll be towing his car to Manteo and we'll find out exactly what he does have in there. And by the way, I've been informed by the higher-ups that there's a bit of a breach in the dune over there," he said, pointing toward Felix's property, "and that there will be more than the usual heavy equipment working to repair it. So, don't be alarmed if you notice anything...shall we say... *unusual*. That's federal land and everything has approval from the top. You understand what I'm tellin' you here?" He looked at both of them knowingly.

"Yes, we understand, David," Annie said. Daniel nodded and thanked him. The Sheriff said goodbye, got in his car and headed south toward the Buxton police department.

Daniel turned to Annie and burst out laughing. "Well, Felix didn't get what he was expecting with that tantrum, did he?"

She grimaced. "Nope, and I hope that I never see his face again! It galls me to no end to think that he's going to profit from the sale of that land!"

"Me, too..." Daniel said. He took her hand and led her over to the porch swing. They sat down and he kept holding her hand. "Whatever happens, I'll support you in every way that I can, Annie. I know a few people in Raleigh who have some influence, and if we need to, we can get some legal help with this."

She looked into his eyes. "Thank you, Daniel. I'm so glad that you've been here for all of this. It would have been overwhelming if I'd had to face it alone, I think. I'm not sure exactly what all is involved here, but I'm just one person and it looks like I'm up against some powerful people in there..." She nodded back toward the house.

"Oh, you'll be fine. You're tough, smart and you haven't done anything wrong – and – Chad said that you'll be handsomely compensated for all your trouble, remember?" He grinned.

"Oh, yeah, I forgot about that part," she said, smiling. "Maybe it won't be so bad after all!"

Chapter 30

Inside, there was a flurry of activity for the rest of the day. Chad came out and told Annie that the two male scientists had reluctantly agreed to share Room 3 when the new guest arrived tomorrow. *Whoever he is,* Annie thought, *he must be important!*

Annie and Daniel stayed out of their way for the rest of the day, taking walks on the beach, sharing tea and getting to know one another even better. She was still shaken by the encounter with Felix, so Daniel tried to comfort her and get her mind off it by making her laugh.

The following day, the scientists got right to work after breakfast. This new person was expected mid-afternoon, so Annie and Terry got the room cleaned and ready and then prepared lunch for the whole gang.

Around four o'clock, a black SUV with darkened windows pulled up into the driveway and parked. Annie looked out the window, pushing the curtains aside. She wasn't sure exactly what she'd expected, but what she actually saw surprised her. A petite brunette with a pixie haircut hopped out of the big vehicle, grabbed her briefcase and strode toward the house.

Annie opened the door and introduced herself. The woman nodded politely, said her name was Jane and asked where the geologists were. Annie pointed toward the closed double doors and said, "I believe that they're expecting you…"

Jane looked Annie over, smiled and said with a soft Southern drawl, "Honey, I do hope that all of us crashin' in on you like this is not gonna be too much for you…" She patted Annie on the arm sympathetically.

Didn't expect that! Annie thought, and she found herself liking Jane right away. "Oh, no, your room is all ready and we'll be just fine. Quarters are a little tight maybe, but we'll make it. Thanks for asking, though."

Jane smiled and Annie noticed how attractive the woman was. Late forties, early fifties maybe, she guessed, and despite her sweetness it was evident that she was a real spitfire. She was a little over five feet tall, but carried herself with the presence of a much larger person. Jane nodded and said, "Well, I assume that they've let you know that you'll be handsomely compensated for all of this?"

Annie nodded. "That's not really necessary; this is my business, it's what I do. My usual fees will be fine."

Jane gave her a 'now-you-know-better-than-that' look, waved her hand dismissively and whispered, "Annie, I don't want to hear another word about *that.* You'll earn every penny of it puttin' up with all those nerdy types. I deal with 'em all the time, and they can be a real pain in the … hiney." She grinned, nodded and headed toward the double doors.

Jane slid both pocket doors open wide, stood there for a moment until the group inside grew silent, put her hands on her hips and said, "Okay, Frank, you and your team of squints here better have a good reason for callin' me all the way down here to the Outer Banks!"

Frank grinned. "Jane, I believe that you'll find we had reason enough! Come on in and I'll introduce you around." Before Jane closed the door, Annie caught a glimpse of the look of respect on the faces of the scientists. Whoever Jane was, she must be a fearful little powerhouse.

Annie went into the kitchen to begin planning tomorrow's breakfast. Daniel came inside later and asked, "Whose big old SUV is that out there?"

Smiling, Annie said, "That's our new guest from Washington."

Daniel whistled low. "He must be somebody important! That's a brand-new Escalade out there, and it looks to be equipped with top-of-the-line everything!"

Annie grinned. "Yep. *She* seems to be somebody important. The scientists all shut right up when she opened the doors." She went back to washing the fruit.

"It's a woman?" He looked surprised.

"Uh-huh. Who were you expecting?" She gave him an innocent look.

He blustered a bit. "Well, I don't know exactly, but... well, she must be somebody important! The plates on the back looked like a government agency, but it also looked kind of, I don't know, secretive," he said, pushing his hair back off his forehead. "I was expecting some type of men-in-black character, I guess..." He laughed.

Annie gave him a look. "She's just a little bit of a thing, but it's clear that she's the person that they're all reporting to. They all stood a little straighter and shut right up when they saw her. Besides, Daniel, don't you remember..." she smiled, "that dynamite comes in small packages?"

Daniel looked impressed. "If she could get all the nerds to shut up by just standing there, well, she must be somebody to be reckoned with!"

"You'd never know it by talking to her. She's got this Southern accent and she's just as sweet as can be. Reminds me a bit of my mom when she was younger." Annie got a faraway look on her face.

Daniel walked to the sink to help her with the fruit. "Yeah, my mom was like that, too. She was sweet, loving and kind, but when she was in charge, we all just got out of her way!"

They shared a few moments talking about their mothers and how much they both missed them. Daniel told her all about the Chinese visitors, complete with Pete's stories about the Mogwai, which had Annie bent over double laughing. When the fruit was all cleaned up and put away, Annie said, "So, you've been hanging out with Finis?" They took a seat at the table.

Daniel laughed. "That old coot! He really raked me over the coals – in his own inimitable way – for my part in all this." He shook his head and grinned. "And yet, at the same time, I get the feeling that he likes me a little..."

"Oh, he likes you alright. But for some reason, he's singled you out to see what you're made of. I can't imagine why; it's just what he does sometimes." She shrugged.

"You think it's because of you?" he asked.

"What do you mean?"

"Well," he said, pushing his hair back, "he can tell that I like you, I think, and he's pretty protective of you in case you hadn't noticed."

"You... like me?" she sputtered.

He looked at her. "Yes, Annie, I like you – a lot. I more-than-like you! I'm hoping that after all our business is done that I can come back and we can get to know each other even better. You're a special woman, and you and I get along like we've known each other all our lives. Don't you think?" He had opened up more than he intended and gave her a very vulnerable look.

She smiled and nodded. "I feel the same way, Daniel. It's just that... well, I have this 'Rule Number One' that I never get involved with a guest, so I haven't really let myself think about it much." She looked a little embarrassed.

"No problem. I can go stay somewhere else," he said, grinning. "Just point me in the direction of the nearest lodgings." He took her hand. "Seriously."

She shook her head. "No, don't go, Daniel, but, well, let me think about this, okay? It's moving kind of fast, and with all this other business going on," she nodded toward the large room where the scientists were, "I'm a bit confused about some things. Be patient with me, please." She gave him her best smile.

He picked up her hand and kissed the top of it softly. "Absolutely."

Suddenly Jane opened the door and walked in. "Well, we – uh, excuse me, please," she said, noticing their intimate moment. "I can come back later." She turned to leave.

Lies in the Sand

"No, stay, please, Jane. This is Daniel Marcus, the appraiser who was sent by his firm to work on the auction for the property next door. Daniel, this is Jane... I didn't get your last name, Jane." She looked inquisitively at her.

"Jones. Jane Jones," she said, smiling. "Really!"

"Nice to meet you, Jane," Daniel said, standing up and walking over to shake her hand. "Please join us." He pointed toward the empty chair at the little table.

Jane appeared to think about it and then smiled. "Ya'll got any coffee around here? After dealing with those scientists and all their high-falutin' talk, I could sure use a cup!"

Annie got up and walked over to the counter. Pouring a cup, she asked, "How do you take it, Jane?"

"Black and powerful, just like my SUV," she teased, and then took the offered cup. "So, you're probably wonderin' what all this ruckus is about, I imagine?" Jane asked, sipping. "Hey, that's good coffee!" she added.

"Thanks," Annie said. "Organic beans, grind them myself. But yes, we have been wondering; Chad and that gang won't tell us anything. Can you?"

Jane took another sip and thought about it. "Well, I can tell you this: that piece of land has some strange properties to it – but ya'll already knew that, I reckon."

"You talking about the magnetic influence that weirds-out compasses?" Daniel asked.

She nodded. "Uh-huh. The nerds have discovered that there's a large 'sumthin' down there that may be causing the effect, and they need to excavate it to find out what it is."

"But why are *you* here?" Annie asked. "You're obviously not a geologist..."

Jane nodded. "Let me just say this: if that thing down there is what they think it might be, your government wants to know all about it. So, they sent me; I'm what you might call a 'specialist' in some areas."

"Are you FBI?" Daniel asked.

She turned to him and grinned. "Not exactly, Honey. But if I told you what it is that I do, then I'd have to wipe your memory." She laughed out loud, slapping the table.

Daniel looked worried. Annie looked stunned.

Jane waved her hand around. "Oh, keep your shorts on, ya'll, I'm just foolin' with ya! Suffice it to say that I work for the federal government and whatever this thing is, we'll all be out of your hair real soon. And Annie, there'll be no damage to your property, I can promise you that." Jane looked serious. "In fact, I can go so far as to say that you'll be quite happy with the outcome, when everything's said and done." She smiled.

Annie took a deep breath and exhaled loudly. "If you say so, Jane…"

Jane nodded. She turned to Daniel. "And your company will be informed shortly that your services will no longer be needed, so you're free to go back to… where is it you came from?"

"Raleigh," Daniel said. "About fours hours west of here. But I don't mind staying as long as you need me," he added sheepishly, glancing at Annie.

Jane sized up the situation quickly. "Hmmm… well, you better stay a few more days, Daniel, just to be sure. I'll phone your boss. No problem." She grinned at them. "Hey, ya'll got any cookies to go with this coffee?"

Chapter 31

That night the whole group went out to a big seafood feast at a nearby restaurant. The proprietors were more than happy to have such a big group at this slow time of year, and gave them great food and excellent personal service. They all sat around eating and drinking until nearly ten.

The following morning everybody got down to business. When Annie woke up, there was a big backhoe over on the property next door. She hadn't even heard it come in; this *was* an efficient operation. A few other pieces of odd-looking equipment stood nearby. Large blue tarps were being hung on either side of the work site, so that from ground level it was impossible to see exactly what was being done. The sounds of digging went on and on.

Late in the morning the digging stopped. Annie noticed that the backhoe was out on the beach and something else seemed to be going on. The scientists came in, ate their lunch quickly and went right back to work. Annie and Daniel went for more groceries and kept themselves busy. Neither of them was allowed on the property while the work was going on. 'Safety concerns' was all they were told. More black SUV's had arrived and four men-in-black types seemed to be hanging around the periphery of the work, carefully keeping watch.

Jane was up and down the beach to the worksite; she'd set up her desk out on the back porch so that she could keep an eye on the work. Most of her time was spent on the phone and computer, but every so often she'd get a text and trot down there to hash something out with the geologists.

The work went on all day, and the workers ordered pizza for dinner so that they wouldn't have to leave. After dark Annie heard a different noise; some kind of large semi-truck had backed onto the property from the road and was making its way toward the beach. Annie could see the lights from the truck until it disappeared into a small stand of trees.

There were more construction sounds until around ten, and then the truck pulled out and headed north on the highway. The SUV with the guard-types followed right behind it. Annie had worried that the big rig might get stuck in the sand, but evidently these guys knew what they were doing because, whatever was happening, it all went off without a hitch. Annie's need for sleep outweighed her curiosity and she went to bed.

The next morning Jane informed her that the crew would be cleaning up the mess today and be gone by tomorrow. When pressed, all she would say was that she would get back to them as soon as possible to let them know as much as she could tell them. Jane stayed until mid-afternoon, packed up her things and found Annie and Daniel on the front porch swing, holding hands.

"Ya'll make such a cute couple," she said, taking a seat in a nearby rocking chair. "How long have you known each other, if you don't mind me asking?"

Annie looked a bit embarrassed, but Daniel spoke right up. "Actually, we only met a little over a week ago," he said. "But I liked her right away!"

Jane nodded. "Okey-dokey, then! Sometimes it doesn't take long at all to figure these things out," she said knowingly. "When I met my husband, I knew the moment I met him that he was the one for me!"

"How did you know?" Annie asked.

Jane laughed. "Well, right off the bat, he didn't shoot me, so I figured that he was smart. He had his gun drawn, he was in a shooting stance, but when we locked eyes..." she smiled. "Let's just say that it was a good thing that we were both on the same side, or there might have been an international incident." She laughed out loud, slapping her thigh. "Imagine this: a girl from Georgia fallin' for a Brit!" She shook her head. "Well, we made it work somehow and neither of us has ever looked back, so it must be true love." She reflected for a moment. "We've had a lot of rivers to cross, but we found out that if the two of you hold hands, it makes treacherous waters a lot easier to get through."

"I love that story!" Annie said. Daniel laughed and nodded. "What else can you tell us?"

Jane thought about it for a long moment and then said, "Well, Honey, I can't go into any details because of the nature of my work, and his, too, but I'll tell you this: if you want to, you can work anything out. You really gotta want to. You gotta want to *real bad* some days, but you can do it if you don't give up!"

She stood up. "I gotta get goin' now, but I promise that I'll be back to see ya'll soon. I might even bring the Brit with me and stay a few days!" She walked over and gave Annie a hug. "Now, don't you worry about anything, Honey, it's all gonna work out, and you'll be just fine – you hear me?"

Annie nodded and smiled. Jane turned and hugged Daniel, too, patting him on the back and whispering in a low voice, "You be good to her. I can be a dangerous woman." His eyes got big, he nodded and then she gave him a big smile. "See ya'll later!" She waved, walked down the steps and hopped up into her big SUV.

"Good thing that big black beast she drives has a running board, or she'd never be able to get into it!" Daniel said, as Jane started it up and drove slowly down the driveway.

Lies in the Sand

Chapter 32

Daniel watched from his upstairs window as the geologists finished up their work. He'd been keeping an eye on them covertly and had seen some things that he didn't understand. Being naturally curious, he determined to find out as much as possible and cornered Chad outside later that morning. "You leaving soon?" he asked.

"Hopefully by tomorrow morning at the latest," Chad answered, "if we can get everything wrapped up."

"So... let me ask you something," Daniel said. "That thing – the big one – that you dug up out there, what was it?"

Chad looked stunned. "What do you mean?"

Daniel shook his head. "Don't play games with me, Chad, the view from my room upstairs is perfect for watching what was going on!"

Chad glanced up and saw that Daniel's window did indeed overlook the work site. He seemed nervous and looked around. "Daniel, don't ever say anything about what you saw to anyone! You didn't see it! Do you understand me? I'm serious about this!"

"Well, it was dark and all and I couldn't see a whole lot, but the lights you had out there made it easy to tell that you had dug up something – in fact, it looked like a couple of somethings – and hauled them off in the middle of the night! That's all I could see..."

Chad took Daniel by the arm and walked down toward the beach, where the sound of the surf drowned out the possibility of anyone overhearing them. "Listen, Daniel, you should *not* know what you know. And if any of those people," he added, nodding toward the group working not far away, "ever found out that you do, it would cause you an endless amount of grief."

He stopped short and poked Daniel in the chest. "In fact, I could get in trouble for not letting them know that you know! But we've been friends for a long time, and I am sure that you're the type of guy who can keep his mouth shut. If you promise me that you'll never utter a word about this to anyone, I'll keep you out of it, but you have to promise! Can you do that? Will you?"

His silly old roommate had suddenly turned hard. Daniel stepped back from his friend. "Seriously, Chad? Are you telling me that this is some kind of government secret, what you found over there?"

Chad stepped forward. "I'm telling you *that nothing was found over there, do you hear me? Nothing!*" His hard look convinced Daniel that something about this was extremely serious, despite it coming from his usually lighhearted friend, Chad.

Daniel swallowed and nodded. "I haven't done anything wrong, you know..."

"Of course you haven't, but there are some things that it is better to stay as far away from as you can get, and this is one of them! If you get involved even a little, your whole life will change, and I don't think you want that, do you?"

Daniel shook his head.

"Okay then, give me your word!"

Daniel swallowed hard. "I... I promise, Chad. I won't ever mention it to another living soul!"

"Especially Annie! You got that?"

"Uh-huh, I sure don't want to do anything to mess her life up! But can you give me some kind of, uh hint about what it was?"

Chad's face was turning red. "No! Absolutely not! And this is the last we will ever speak of it, you got it?"

Lies in the Sand

Daniel was beginning to understand the seriousness of this situation. "Okay, I understand. Nothing. Ever. To anyone. I give you my word!"

Chad seemed to relax a little. "Alright then. We never had this conversation. You go back to Raleigh and check in with your boss and forget you were ever here." He stared at his friend and made a face. "Well, you could come back for... personal reasons, I suppose, if you want to. But no business!"

Daniel grinned. "I intend to come back for personal reasons – and soon, Chad! I really like Annie, and I believe the feeling's mutual. We have to see where this thing goes."

Chad nodded and visibly softened. "Of course, you do. And I'm sure that it'll never be a problem if you keep your word. Silence. Forever." He gave his friend a final forbidding look.

"Forever," Daniel said.

The two of them walked back toward the house, now chatting about old friends and other innocent things. Had it not been for the intensity of that last few minutes of conversation, Daniel could almost imagine the whole incident had never happened.

Lies in the Sand

Chapter 33

Chad informed Annie that they would all be gone by the next morning, and that would give her a day to get the place ready for her next guests. He thanked her profusely and informed her that, as long as she didn't talk about what had gone on with the scientists, there would be a generous reward in it for her.

Annie could easily comply because she didn't really *know* what had gone on, other than that they'd been digging around over there, so she agreed. No doubt some of the nosey neighbors would be wanting to pump her for all the information they could get, but it would be easy to say that the scientists had just been some nerds on vacation, nothing to it. And the digging, well that was just some heavy equipment brought in to reinforce one of the dunes that had been breached. That kind of thing went on all the time up and down this seashore.

The two women scientists pulled out that evening, and Chad and the two men shortly after breakfast the next morning. That left Frank and Daniel. They sat talking with Annie over coffee after the others had cleared out.

"I do hope that you'll come back and visit again, Frank," Annie said, patting his hand. "It's been nice having you as a guest, and Finis thinks the world of you!"

He laughed. "That Finis is certainly a character! Under that good-ole-boy exterior, he's actually very wise – and a little bit cunning, too," he added, looking at Daniel. "And in case you're wondering, Daniel, he's decided that, to put it as he did, 'you'll do.' Coming from him, that's about as good as you'll get, I think." He grinned at both of them. "And yes, Annie, I'd love to come back and bring my wife. I'll be retiring in a few years and promised her a lot of travel, so we'll be coming to see you often, I'm sure."

"Wonderful!" Annie said. "You're always welcome. Just call ahead and I'll give you the best room upstairs – the one you gave up for Jane." She smiled and shook her head. "Jane, now there's a character! She's like a sugar-coated piece of dynamite – I never saw anybody snap to attention like ya'll did when she showed up!"

Frank nodded. "She's a formidable woman, but you're right about the sugar part. It's that sweet side of her that's kept the powers that be from messing with her. She has the President's ear – and not just this one, all of them for the last fifteen years! But you didn't hear that from me, did you?" They both shook their heads. "Well, I better go. Thanks for everything!" He stood up and headed upstairs to finish packing.

"I suppose that I have to leave, too…" Daniel said, looking down. "Wish I could stay longer, but life and work goes on." He looked up at Annie and grinned. "Now that I've got your phone number, you won't be able to get away from me."

She smiled sweetly. "I'm not complaining. And if you lose the number, it's listed, just Google it. You better keep in touch!"

Daniel put his bag down beside the door. He walked up to Annie and tentatively gave her a hug. She melted against him, feeling that this might be exactly where she belonged. She looked up at him and he smiled. Annie reached up, touched the side of his face and kissed him. He stood there grinning like an idiot.

"Come back soon, Daniel," she said as she let him go.

"That's all I needed to hear, Annie," he said, picking up his suitcase and walking on to the porch. He looked around, took a deep breath and said quietly, "Oh, yeah. I'll be back." Waving as he went down the stairs, he moved toward his car and got in.

Annie came running down the steps and up to his car window. He rolled it down and looked at her curiously. "Just one more thing, Daniel," she said. Grabbing him by the front of his shirt, she pulled him in for another long kiss. "Make it soon, you hear me?" she said. He nodded and she ran back inside.

You bet! he told himself. Soon, indeed!

Chapter 34

Raleigh, NC, one month later

Daniel noticed the name of the caller and answered his phone. "Hey, Beautiful, nice of you to call in the middle of the day like this! Just couldn't wait to hear my voice, could you?"

Annie laughed. "No need to get excited, now, I just need to run something past you real quick. Got a minute?"

"For you, of course! What's up?"

Annie hesitated before saying, "Well, I got a phone call from Jane Jones – you remember her, right?"

"Oh, yeah, who could forget that little dynamo? What did she want?"

"She made a reservation for herself and her husband – 'the Brit', she called him – for this weekend. They're coming in tomorrow night..."

"Okay. Well, I suppose she really liked it at the *Sandy Bottom*. But what's on your mind?"

"I got a feeling from talking to her that it's more than R&R, that she's coming for a reason. Now, I'm not quite sure about that part, but if she is, I'd like for you to be here. Do you think you could manage another long weekend on the Outer Banks?"

He heard the smile in her voice. "There's nothing I'd like more! In fact, I can leave after lunch tomorrow because it's a slow week and Ron won't mind. I'll be there by five at the latest."

"Wonderful! Can't wait to see you, Daniel! And thanks for humoring me on this."

"Hey, any time you get the irresistible urge to have me around, all you have to do is call, Beautiful, and I'll be there!"

She laughed. "Now don't get all proud of your irresistible self! I'll see you tomorrow!"

Chapter 35

Daniel had already arrived and unpacked his suitcase when Jane and her husband drove up. He and Annie were sitting on the front porch swing together holding hands again. They waved as the little woman turned off the big black SUV and hopped out. The passenger door opened and an average looking man in his fifties got out and walked around to get the luggage.

"He doesn't look so scary!" Daniel whispered.

"Neither does she, but do you remember how those scientists shaped up when she got here?" Annie replied. Daniel nodded.

"Well, if that's not the purtiest picture I ever saw!" Jane said, climbing the steps to the porch. "You two look like you belong together in that swing!" Her effervescent personality was in full force. She turned around and yelled at her husband. "Now be sure to git all of it!" He looked up, gave her a look and then began to trudge toward the house with the suitcases.

Daniel hopped up and went down to help him. "Daniel Marcus," he said as he took two of the cases. "Welcome to the *Sandy Bottom B&B*!"

"Right-O, thank you kindly," the man replied. "Geoff Jones, pleasure to meet you, Daniel," he replied, shook his hand and then followed him toward the house. On the porch, the two women were hugging and chatting away. Daniel looked back at Geoff, who simply rolled his eyes.

Once they got settled in their room, the couple came back downstairs. "Now, we're taking you both out for dinner tonight, and that's all there is to it – no arguments, you hear?" Jane said, grinning.

Lies in the Sand

"No, you don't have to – " Annie began.

"I wouldn't argue with her if I were you, my dear," her husband said. "You don't want to make her angry, trust me." He gave them a bit of a smile. His wife looked at him with love in her eyes and then punched him in the upper arm.

"Don't pay any attention to him!" Jane said. "He hated that long drive down here from Washington and he's in a grumpy mood. These Europeans think every place they want to go should be within a two-hour drive! After he eats, he'll be nicer." She nodded and gave them a knowing look.

"I say, Darling, that's very nearly a compliment!" he said to her. She smiled and snuggled close to him. They took a quick walk on the beach, then came back in and got ready to go for dinner. The four of them enjoyed a lovely meal, some good wine and a lot of conversation.

During the meal, Jane informed them that they wouldn't be having any more trouble from the owner of the property, Felix Benefield. The local police, and then later the feds, had settled him down with some time behind bars, so he was a lot more agreeable these days.

The lawyers explained to him that the Federal Government had acquired his property back in the 1950's when they formed the National Seashore. Evidently, no one had been able to locate the owner at the time, so it was condemned and seized as public domain. The title deed had belonged to the U.S. government for over sixty years now, and there was zero chance that Benefield would be getting his hands on it.

Jane added, "Benefield demanded compensation, so they sent him a check for $1,200, which they said was a generous estimate of the worth of the property back in 1954 and told him never to question it again. They suggested that his lifetime of IRS returns might just be pulled up and each one audited with a fine-tooth comb if he gave them any trouble." She smiled. "He's stupid, but not crazy. He'll leave it alone and probably stay out of the country for a long while!"

Annie and Daniel laughed and hugged each other. "So much for his big windfall!" she said.

Lies in the Sand

"Oh, and one other thing..." Jane said. "If you decide to put up a firepit and a gazebo over on that land like you'd mentioned, the government will have no objection at all. I've seen to it. You don't have to worry about anyone else ever messin' around with the land; the paperwork's in the hands of the U.S. government, and ya'll know how secure that is! It'll probably be filed away in some dusty digital warehouse and never be seen again!" She gave them her best innocent look.

The next morning, they lingered over breakfast. The other guests had left to go sight-seeing so it was just the four of them. Annie said, "Well, I better get this cleaned up. There's work to do," she said as she began to stand up.

Jane put her hand over Annie's. "Stay for a little while, Honey. I have some other things to tell you. And you, too, Daniel." Annie nodded and sat down.

"When I was here a few months back and we did the excavation," she began, "there was a lot of hush-hush stuff goin' on and I couldn't tell you anything about it. I'm sure it must have seemed strange to you. But now that's all sorted out, and I wanted to let you in on a few developments." She paused for a moment to collect her thoughts.

"What kind of things did you dig up?" Annie asked innocently.

Jane raised an eyebrow. "Things? How many things do you think we took out of that hole?"

Daniel kept quiet and tried not to show any reaction. After all, Annie had not been privy to the conversation he'd had with Chad, so her question was a natural one.

"Oh, I don't know," Annie said, shrugging. "Just seemed like there was a lot of digging going on for a little while there. Surely you found something?"

Jane nodded. "Yes, there was a lot of digging, but we didn't uncover anything important or of value, other than historical. That's what I wanted to tell you about: we dug up an old wooden chest that the experts say is probably from the 1700's."

Lies in the Sand

Annie looked at Daniel and said, "So, maybe *that is* Blackbeard's lost treasure that there are so many stories about? Could it be?"

Jane smiled. "There was no way to positively identify it with any particular person, but they say that the time is about right for it to be Blackbeard's. This area was his hangout as well, so that backs up the theory. The historians are pretty sure that it belonged to him, they just can't prove it at this point."

"Was it full of treasure?" Daniel asked, leaning forward. "Gold, gems, that kind of thing?"

Jane looked at her husband and then laughed. "Well, that's the funny part of the story. There were several rotting cloth bags in there, and after the scientists analyzed the contents, they determined that there had just been powder in those bags!"

"Powder! What kind of treasure is that?" Annie exclaimed.

Jane shook her head. "Nowadays it would be worth almost nothing, but back in those times, that powder would have brought a hefty price anywhere there was malaria, and that was a lot of places! It was powdered chinchona bark mostly, which contains quinine; it was used to treat heart conditions and known as the best medicine to treat malaria. It was also called 'Jesuits' bark' or 'Peruvian bark' because it was discovered in the high mountains of Peru and introduced by Jesuit priests in the 1600's as a cure."

"Quinine?" Daniel asked. "Plain old quinine was valuable?"

Geoff spoke up. "In the 17th and 18th centuries, London apothecaries stocked it, but only for their exclusive patients who could afford it. The stuff was that dear. Only the rich had the means to pay for it. So, if someone managed to procure a big lot of the stuff, he would have been a rich man!"

"So how did Blackbeard – or whoever owned the chest – get his hands on it?" Annie asked.

Jane shrugged. "The historians believe that it came from some Spanish trading ships that were carrying it to the New World to sell. They must have been plundered by pirates, or else it would have made its way there safely and been sold..."

Daniel laughed. "So, Blackbeard's priceless treasure was a pile of herb dust?"

"To be precise," Geoff said, "it comes from the bark of trees. But basically, that is correct. And it would have made whoever owned it a rich man if he took it to the southern colonies, the Caribbean, the tropics, or even the far east. In fact, it's said that the Japanese emperor was healed by the powder. The British officers in India often added a little of it to a mixture of water, sugar, lime and gin to ward off malaria. So, the next time you have a gin-and-tonic old boy, remember to thank the Peruvian monks!"

Everyone laughed. "Yes, and we'll say 'here's to Blackbeard!', too!" Daniel said, lifting his coffee cup. "But – that still doesn't explain the strange effect the property had on a compass, does it? And, before you say anything, let me tell you that Annie and I have checked that out already, and – whatever was causing that – it's gone. A compass points true north now over there, and we couldn't figure out what had changed. What happened?" He recalled seeing the large objects lifted into the truck but wasn't going to say anything about it because he'd given Chad his word.

Jane looked a bit uncomfortable but then she smiled. "Actually, there was a good-sized meteorite underneath the chest. They're still analyzing it, but at this point they've found that it's very high in magnetite, maghemite and pyrrhotite, along with a few unknown minerals. All of those have a magnetic effect and can throw off a compass. Evidently, the combination of the three put off a pretty strong magnetic field, they tell me. So, mystery solved!"

"Maybe that was why the pirate buried the treasure there – so he could find it again easily with a compass," Annie said.

Jane nodded. "Good point." She gave them both a serious look. "Now, the part about the meteorite is something that you can't mention to anyone. I only told you because you were here and you deserve an explanation for the strange magnetic effect. As far as anyone else knows, all we dug up is the old chest full of dusty powder. You understand?"

"Of course!" Daniel said.

Annie nodded. "But why keep the meteorite a secret? Those things come down all over the place."

Geoff spoke up. "At this point, the exact composition of the rock is still a mystery, and we don't want a flood of crazies coming down and trying to dig up your lovely beach to try to snag themselves a piece. Someone might believe that it's valuable, which it probably is not."

"Oh, I hadn't thought of that, good idea," Annie said.

Daniel on the other hand, wasn't quite buying that explanation. "What about the treasure? Don't you think that people will come and try to dig up some more treasure over there when they find out where the chest came from?"

Jane shook her head. "The only description given will be that it was found on the Outer Banks, and that's a large hunk of real estate! As far as the chest and its contents go, it will go into the Smithsonian after all the squints are done analyzing it to death." She rolled her eyes. "Scientists! They make mountains out of mole hills every time! But I suppose it'll be considered a real historical find, and the museum is anxious to get it. They intend to make it a part of their 'Pirates in the Atlantic' collection and play it up as the treasure that it once was. Should cause quite a stir with all the pirate fanatics running around today!"

"Do I see another Jack Sparrow movie in our future?" Annie asked, grinning.

Jane snorted. "Oh, for Pete's sake, I hope not! Every time I see that character he reminds me of Pepe Le Pew, the French lover-boy cartoon skunk, remember him? I can't take the story seriously because I keep picturing Johnny Depp as Pepe saying something like 'Zee game of love eez never called on account of darkness'!" She rolled her eyes and made a face.

All four of them laughed out loud. Annie finally wiped her eyes and said, "Yes, I remember Pepe, and now that you mention it, I'll never be able to see Jack Sparrow the same again!"

Lies in the Sand

Jane said, "Well, I'll help you clean up, and then we can all do some sightseein', okay? I want to see that museum. What's it called?"

"Chicamacomico," Daniel answered. "And you'll love it! Those men were true heroes, and almost nobody has heard of them. It's something to see – what they had to do back in the day to save people from shipwrecks!"

They all got up and started clearing the table. Annie and Daniel took the dishes into the kitchen. Geoff pulled Jane aside and asked quietly, "Do you think they believed the bit about the meteorite?"

She nodded and smiled. "Why not? It's as good a cover story as any."

He shrugged. "I suppose so. Nice touch, Darling." He tweaked her under the chin and she winked at him.

"Let's get going," Annie called out from the kitchen. "You'll want to spend some time at the museum."

"Okay, Sweetie," Jane said, and smiled at her husband.

Lies in the Sand

Chapter 36

Somewhere in the Nevada desert

The unremarkable semi-truck rolled down the pavement on Route 375, a road which had been renamed by the locals as the "Alien Highway." Powerful semis pulling trailers behind were a common site in the area, as on most highways out west, so no one thought anything about the big rig rolling along.

Two casually dressed men inside the cab of the truck appeared to be perfectly normal truck drivers. They kept a close eye on the rear-view mirrors, even though no traffic had been seen for hours on this lonely stretch of pavement except for their escort vehicle behind them. In the middle of the night, on a lonely desert road, no traffic was expected. A helicopter also followed slowly, far enough back to keep an eye on the truck but not close enough to be associated with it.

As the driver Matt, downshifted, his partner Tim watched the GPS signal closely. "Go even slower. It's only a hundred yards more. On the left," Tim said. Matt nodded. He turned the big rig onto a gravel road and drove for miles until they came to a tall chain-link fence which stretched for miles in both directions. There was no closed or locked gate across the road there, but on either side, were signs declaring this to be a U.S. Air Force Installation ('PHOTOGRAPHY OF THIS AREA IS PROHIBITED'), though no specific name was given for the base.

Lies in the Sand

Several huge red stop-signs didn't deter the drivers; they simply drove right through the gate without slowing down, the black van following right behind them. An imposing security camera setup filmed their approach and transmitted the signal, but no one tried to stop them. In fact, no guards or guard booths were to be seen. However, if you went past the stop-signs, guards with heavy weapons would quickly appear and bring you to a sudden halt within a few hundred yards, if you didn't have proper authorization.

The locals knew all of this and gave the place a wide berth, although alien-hunting tourists routinely walked up to the gates. Even in the daylight, there was really nothing to see from that point except desert and the occasional monotonous rolling hill dotted here and there with scrubby trees.

Tourists could get a lot more information at the nearby motels and restaurants. Most of it was fiction of course, but it filled the need and gave the small town an endless stream of curious visitors seeking proof of extraterrestrials and the location of 'Area 51'.

After a few more miles, lights began to descend slowly from the sky. Tim said to the Matt, "Looks like the 'Janet' transport is earlier than usual today. I bet those workers at McCarran hate to get up for this shift!" They both laughed as the commuter airline plane came into a graceful landing nearby.

"Yep. And you know that they're not paid nearly what we are," the driver added, and they laughed some more.

The truck arrived at a run-down looking warehouse just as dawn began to break. The driver stopped and waited. A crew came out to meet the rig. At the same time, six heavily armed soldiers piled out of the black van, scanning the area carefully. They walked behind and beside the truck as Matt backed the rig backed up to a loading dock. The armed men quickly set up a perimeter around the truck and took up a defensive posture.

After shutting off the engine, Matt wondered aloud, "Why didn't they just put some of the guards in with the package like they usually do? Why the need for a follow-up vehicle?"

Lies in the Sand

"Good question. I heard somebody back in Virginia mention something about radiation or exposure or something like that I think...might be hazardous." Tim shrugged.

The driver jerked his head around. "*Radiation*? Why didn't you warn me? Have we been exposed, you think?" He got a worried look on his face. "Will it have any effect on my... you know..."

"Probably not, they usually take precautions about that kind of stuff. I wouldn't worry about it..." Tim answered casually. The driver still appeared quite unsettled when a soldier stepped up to his door with a paper requiring his signature and shoved it at him. Matt signed and handed it back to him, but said nothing.

The Sargent with the clipboard stared at him. "You okay, airman? You look like somebody just shot your dog! You sick or something?"

Matt opened his mouth to ask about radiation, but before he could say anything, Tim answered for him. "No sir, just tired from driving all night, that's all."

The guard gave both of them an intensive looking-over. "Alright then. Head over to the barracks, get yourself something to eat and grab some sleep. We'll be reloading the truck for your return trip. Be back by eleven hundred hours."

"Yes, sir!" they both snapped and saluted. The two men got out of the cab and walked over to another nondescript building a few hundred yards away, checked in with the guard and then entered a double door leading to an already busy mess hall.

They looked at one another as they entered the noisy room. "I still don't like it," Matt said. "Being exposed to some kind of weird radiation, I mean. I ain't no guinea pig!"

"Nuthin' we can do about it now, is there?" Tim answered, shrugging.

Matt thought about that. "Guess not. But if for some reason I can't have kids one day, the Air Force is going to hear about it!" he said, straightening his back.

The other man guffawed. "And you think the Air Force is going to take the blame for *that?*" He doubled over laughing. Matt gave Tim a dirty look.

As they walked, the driver shook his head slowly and heaved a sigh. *All in a day's work. I suppose that's why they pay us so well...* he thought as he walked up to the cafeteria line and grabbed a tray. He spotted some good-looking bacon and put that worrisome thought out of his mind as he decided what else he wanted for breakfast this morning.

Back at the loading dock, the large crates had been transferred to the cargo elevator. Two soldiers got in the elevator to go down with the first load. One asked, "So where does this batch go?"

The other soldier glanced at the paperwork. "All the way down to *The Bottom*." They gave each other a look.

"If you say so," the other soldier said, standing a little straighter. "Man, I sure do hate going down there!"

"Me, too! But whatcha gonna do?"

"You ever bring anything up from there?"

"Nope. If they move any of that junk out of here, they get somebody else to do it, I guess. As far as I know things go down there, but nuthin' ever comes out!"

They both shrugged and then one pushed the bottom button on the panel. Whatever was in those crates was Top Secret. It wasn't every day that they went all the way down... to **Warehouse 13**.

Chapter 37

Before heading back to Raleigh, Daniel took Annie's hand and kissed her palm softly. "Would you consider it harassment if I came back next weekend?" he asked, smiling.

She reached up and put her arms around his neck. "I'd consider it neglect if you waited much longer..." She kissed him.

"Well, somebody needs to protect you from 'the curse' and all that... so I guess I'd better make it my job!" he said seriously.

She laughed. "If I see any suspicious-looking pirate types, I'll consider it an emergency and phone you immediately!"

He kissed her one last time. "Well, there may be no 'Blackbeards' around here, but I'm hoping that I'll be hanging around until I'm a 'graybeard' at least..."

She hugged him tight. "I like the sound of that, Daniel Marcus!"

Finis stood across the road and watched the two of them canoodling on the porch. He grunted and said to nobody in particular, "I guess he'll do." He let slip a little smile and turned for home.

THE END

Lies in the Sand

Lies in the Sand

The legend of Blackbeard's 'buried treasure' somewhere on the Outer Banks is still very much alive. A shipwreck fitting the time period and the description of his flagship *Queen Anne's Revenge*, was discovered in the shallows off the coast of North Carolina in 1996.

Items recovered from the wreck so far include: large cannons, personal items, and about one ounce of gold dust. So, from the evidence recovered so far, if Blackbeard did have a huge booty and this was his ship, the treasure very well could be buried somewhere nearby. The wreck looks to have gone down slowly, so Blackbeard could have offloaded all the cargo from it onto the smaller ships in his fleet before it sank. But then... who knows?

Before you grab your gear and go treasure-hunting, keep in mind that the Outer Banks is about two hundred miles long; and if you added all the ins and outs of every inlet, the actual shoreline could be many hundreds of miles longer than that! So, be prepared to stay a while when you come visit!

Thank you to my Readers for sharing this story with me! If you enjoy my books, please tell your friends who like to read clean, uplifting, intriguing stories.

And if you have a moment, please leave me a review on amazon.com or one of the other book review sites. That really helps an independent author like me, and I'd sure appreciate it.

Please visit my website, **sharronfrink.com**, for more information on each of my novels and feel free to contact me!

Sharron Frink

Lies in the Sand

Made in the USA
Middletown, DE
21 April 2019